London – and young throne of England throws open a whole new world to Deborah Wyngarde and her brother Philip. The overthrow of Parliament's harsh rule means that their exiled father can return to England, and that they can take their rightful places as heirs to a barony. But their thrilling journey to the capital seems wasted when they learn that their father is dead, their inheritance claimed by a cousin. Danger dogs the Wyngardes' footsteps, and Deborah promptly loses her heart to Charles, Earl of Mulgarth – whom even his own sister declares to be nothing but a hardened rake!

Stolen Inheritance
Anne Madden

MILLS & BOON LIMITED
London · Sydney · Toronto

*First published in Great Britain 1980
by Mills & Boon Limited, 17–19 Foley Street,
London W1A 1DR*

© Anne Madden 1980
Australian copyright 1980
Philippine copyright 1980

ISBN 0 263 73221 5

The text of this publication or any part thereof may not be reproduced or transmitted in any form or by any means, electronic or mechanical, including photocopying, recording, storage in an information retrieval system, or otherwise, without the written permission of the publisher.

This book is sold subject to the condition that it shall not, by way of trade or otherwise, be lent, resold, hired out or otherwise circulated without the prior consent of the publisher in any form of binding or cover other than that in which it is published and without a similar condition including this condition being imposed on the subsequent purchaser.

Filmset in 10 on 11pt Plantin

*Made and printed in Great Britain by
C. Nicholls & Company Ltd
The Philips Park Press, Manchester*

CHAPTER ONE

THE interior of the stage-coach was hot and stuffy, the seats uncompromisingly hard. With each turn of the wheels, dust rose in clouds, drifting in through the unglazed windows.

To Deborah Wyngarde, seated beside her brother Philip, the journey seemed endless, and their progress along Watling Street agonisingly slow on this, her first visit to London.

Philip had tried to dissuade her from accompanying him, saying it would be far better if he went alone. Summer was the worst time of year in which to visit the capital. She, who had spent all her life in the country, would scarcely be able to breathe in the foetid atmosphere of the crowded city, with its open laystalls, and stinking kennels choked with every conceivable kind of refuse. He knew. He had been there before.

He had pointed out that it was bound to be packed to suffocation. People were flocking to London every day, now that the King had been restored to his throne. There would be a shortage of accommodation. For himself, he did not mind; but he could not expect his sister to sleep in some bug-infested attic. . . .

To all of which Deborah had turned a deaf ear. She had set her heart on going with him, and nothing he could say would make the least difference.

So here she was, attired in her second-best gown of dove grey, feeling uncomfortably hot and not a little sick. Philip had warned her about the swaying motion of the coach, but she had not expected it to be quite as bad as this.

To take her mind off it, she thought once again of the purpose of their visit – to find their father, Lord Wyngarde, whom they had not seen since a certain eventful day in 1646, fourteen years ago. At that time, she had been a child of four, and Philip nine years old.

England had been torn by Civil War. Lord Wyngarde had fought for the King; his cousin Francis for Parliament. There had never been any love lost between the two men. With the Royalist armies scattered and decimated, Lord Wyngarde, pursued by the cousin who hated him, had been forced to flee for his life. A brief, poignant farewell to his wife and children, and then he was gone.

Deborah had only a faint recollection of him – a tall man with steady grey eyes, his brown hair worn in Cavalier curls. Philip bore a marked resemblance to him, but *she* had inherited her mother's looks – hair the colour of ripe corn and eyes grey-blue beneath winged brows. Though she was not vain, she was nevertheless glad that her brows and lashes were dark, and her skin smooth and unblemished.

Lady Wyngarde, warned beforehand of the coming of the Roundheads, had sent Philip and Deborah to safety in the care of their nurse, Mattie, and another servant, Luke. They had gone to her cousin, John Ryall, who owned a small manor house near the secluded little village of Hallowden, several miles away.

Luke, returning cautiously next day to their own home, Wyngarde Court, had found one wing almost completely burnt out. In the rest of the house the lovely carved panelling had been hacked and torn apart, windows shattered, doors forced from their hinges, furniture smashed, hangings ripped to shreds.

Clearly Francis Wyngarde, having failed to find his quarry, had ordered his men to sack the place. There was little doubt the whole building would have been burnt to the ground, had not a heavy fall of rain quenched the flames.

That was bad enough, but there was worse to come. Lady Wyngarde was dead. Driven out to seek what shelter she could, she had met her death that same night, thrown from the horse on which she had been riding pillion behind one of her husband's tenants, on her way to Hallowden.

Even then it seemed that Francis's vindictive hate had not

been fully appeased. He had set his men to scour the countryside for the two children, with the intention of using them as hostages to force their father to give himself up. But the search was unsuccessful.

A month later, a bout of army fever had struck down many in the district, including two children whose bodies had been identified as those of Philip and Deborah Wyngarde. The man who had identified them had been Luke, swearing on oath, unblinkingly, that he spoke the truth.

Hallowden had been their home, and that of Luke and Mattie, for the past fourteen years. For safety's sake they had taken the name "Ryall", and no one outside the household knew their true identity. The Wyngarde estate had been seized by Parliament, the revenues swelling its coffers.

Of their father they had heard little, save that he had managed to escape to France. He had lived in exile all these years, knowing that his wife was dead and doubtless believing his children to be dead also. What would he say when he found they were alive? Children no longer – Philip had turned twenty-three, she eighteen.

Cousin John, a bachelor, had brought them up as best he could on a limited income. When he had died, a year ago, he had left everything to them, apart from legacies to his servants. The small estate brought them in enough on which to live in reasonable comfort, but with little to spare for luxuries.

One day perhaps, Deborah thought, they would dress in fine clothes, travel in their own coach, have a retinue of servants. One day; when their father came back. That had been their dream through the long years of the Interregnum. Now, at last, the dream might become reality.

How excited they had been at the news of the King's restoration! It meant that their father would be free to return. But when Philip and Luke had ridden over to Wyngarde Court recently, they had found the place still empty, and no one in the district seemed to know anything of Lord Wyngarde's whereabouts.

It was this that had decided Philip to go to London. Their

father had owned a house in Long Street, seized by the
Parliamentarians at the beginning of the war for use as a
lodging for visiting diplomats. If Lord Wyngarde had
returned from exile, he reasoned, he would surely be found
there, near the Court at Whitehall.

Philip had seen the house when he had accompanied
Cousin John on brief visits to the capital. London then had
been a drab city, the people sullen and withdrawn beneath
the yoke of Puritanism and the oppression of Cromwell's
Parliament. It would be different now. Cromwell was dead,
his Parliament tumbled down into the dust. London had
come to life once more.

Deborah wondered momentarily what had happened to
Francis Wyngarde. Their paths had never crossed since the
war. She knew he had a wife and son, and that his home was
somewhere in Buckinghamshire. She hoped the years had
mellowed him. . . .

She gave a little sigh. The gentleman seated opposite her
smiled encouragingly.

"We have only a few more miles to go."

A pleasant gentleman, this, attired in a suit of fine broadcloth, and with a heady aura of heliotrope perfume hanging
about him. He had boarded the coach, as they had, at the
commencement of the journey at St. Albans. His prominent
blue eyes, travelling over Deborah, had registered approval,
and he had at once set himself to charm her, much to Philip's
annoyance. From his conversation, Deborah gathered that
the stranger had been in Hertfordshire on business, though
what manner of business it was, he did not disclose.

Philip had already warned her to guard her own tongue,
not wishing her to discuss their private affairs with all and
sundry. As though she needed to be told! Had he had *his* way,
she would have sat as mute as a post for the duration of the
journey; or at least confined her remarks to him alone.
Always protective towards her, he would be a watchful guardian during their sojourn in London.

She knew she should feel thankful for his care of her, yet
could not help feeling a surge of resentment. She was no

longer a child, nor was she a timid little rabbit, ready to swoon at the least sign of trouble. She had an inherent streak of independence and a keen zest for life, coupled with the joyous optimism of youth.

There was so much to be thankful for – the dreary years at an end, their father free to come home, and they themselves able at last to take their rightful place in the world. . . .

Her eyes danced, and the smile she bestowed upon the friendly gentleman was positively dazzling. His eyes devoured her. She was without doubt the most bewitching little piece he'd ever had the good fortune to meet. A pity their acquaintance seemed doomed to end so soon. Her brother would take good care of that! Seeing that the latter was gazing out of the window, he leaned forward towards Deborah.

"May I ask where you will be staying during your visit to London?"

She lowered her gaze demurely. "I am not sure. My brother knows the address."

"Indeed?" He was momentarily disappointed; then – "If you are strangers to the capital, I should be only too happy to direct you. . . ."

"That will not be necessary." Philip's words cut decisively across the other's. He turned to Deborah. "If you look out of the window, you will soon catch your first glimpse of London."

Dutifully obeying him, she caught sight of a dark smudge on the horizon, a hazy greyness in the otherwise clear sky of the late afternoon – the pall of smoke that lay over the tall spires, the myriad roofs, the tree-lined squares, the shining ribbon of the river.

There had been a fair amount of traffic on the road ever since they had left St. Albans that morning, and now it was becoming more and more congested. There were private coaches, gilded and elegantly panelled, with attendant outriders and postillions; slow, lumbering carriers' carts, conveying both goods and passengers, with their drivers walking beside them, whips in hand; strings of heavily-laden pack-horses; drovers, with straggling herds of cows and flocks of sheep, bound for Smithfield; riders of post-horses. Travellers on foot trudged along the grass verges, covered from head to toe in the dust raised by the passing vehicles.

With the increased traffic the progress of the coach became even slower, until it seemed to Deborah to be no more than a snail's pace along the highway. At last they came within sight of Aldersgate. The coach driver manoeuvred his cumbersome vehicle through the great gate with its attendant stone figures of Jeremiah and Samuel, the heavy iron wheels jarring over the cobblestones.

Deborah felt a thrill of excitement run through her. Looking eagerly out at the busy street, she was soon made aware of the truth of at least *one* of Philip's gloomy prophecies, as the stench of rotting refuse assailed her nostrils. Hastily she buried her nose in her kerchief.

The air was rent with street-cries. "What d'ye lack?" "Come buy my whitings!" "Pease! Pease!" "Lavender – come buy my sweet lavender!" Costard-mongers extolled the virtues of their fruit; tinkers called for pots and pans to mend; water-carriers passed by with their carts . . . a bewildering procession of hawkers, each doing his best to vie with the others. To one used to the peace and quiet of a country village, the noise was deafening.

Almost before she realised it, the coach had lurched into the yard of the Bull and Mouth Inn, where it discharged its passengers. Deborah's admirer handed her down with a gallant bow, managing to keep her hand in his slightly longer than was necessary. While they waited for their cloakbags to be unloaded, he again offered his services as a guide, and was again promptly cut short by Philip.

"Thank you, but a hired coach will suit our purpose admirably."

Even this did not quench the stranger's apparently inexhaustible determination to attach himself to them. At the street corner, where stood the rank of coaches awaiting hire, he was still beside them, ready to assist Deborah into the first one, his hand beneath her elbow.

She thanked him sweetly. Hat in hand, he bowed low, insensible to the look Philip flashed at him as, having given the direction to the driver, he climbed into the coach beside Deborah and slammed the door.

"I hope that's the last we see of *him*!" Philip said grimly, as the hackney moved away. "If you are going to encourage every Tom, Dick and Harry you meet, I shall regret having brought you with me!"

"That's most unfair! I *didn't* encourage him. Why, he was old enough to be my father!"

Philip snorted. "I'll warrant his intentions towards *you* were anything but fatherly! 'Twas a pity he heard the direction I gave the driver. He'd not be above following us."

The address was the one at which he and Mr. Ryall had stayed when visiting London – the sign of the Golden Peacock in Holborn. Here the stout, good-natured landlady, Mrs. Goffin, made them welcome.

"To be sure, 'tis young Mr. Ryall! I remember you well, sir. And this is your sister. Your first visit to London, my dear? I bid you welcome. . . ."

Yes, she could offer them the accommodation they sought – two bedchambers adjoining each other, and a small private parlour. It so happened these were the only empty rooms in the house.

"London's as full of folk as a dog with fleas," she declared, leading the way upstairs. "All come to see the King, bless him!"

"Have *you* seen him, Mrs. Goffin?" asked Deborah eagerly.

Mrs. Goffin beamed at her. "To be sure I have! On the day he entered London. The twenty-ninth of May, it was; and I heard tell it was his thirtieth birthday, too! You never saw such a sight in your life – thousands of people, all in their finest array, and shouting and cheering; the streets decked out with garlands and banners. Then the procession! Why, it took hours to pass us. Then at last came the King, smiling and bowing from his horse, *and* taking his hat off to us, too!

He walks every day in St. James's Park for all to see; and plays at pall-mall and tennis, and rides. . . ."

She had to pause for breath before she could show them into their rooms. "There you are, sir. I trust as they'll suit your purpose. You'll find them clean, and the beds newly-dressed and aired, *and* no fleas or bed-bugs in 'em, neither!"

"I'm sure of it," Philip said. "Yes, these will suit admirably."

The next morning, having breakfasted upon slices of cold beef and bread washed down with ale, they sallied forth upon their quest. Philip had sent the pot-boy for a coach, and away they went towards St. James's.

Both were clad in their best array: Deborah in blue taffeta with a broad collar of much-treasured fine lace, a pearl brooch set in gold pinned at the neck; Philip in a plain but well-cut doublet of dark grey broadcloth, with breeches to match tied at the knee with red ribbons, his legs encased in a pair of silk stockings bought specially for the London venture. They each wore shoes of black leather trimmed with ribbon rosettes.

Deborah went bare-headed, the strings of her travelling cloak loosely tied across her throat. Philip wore a black, broad-brimmed hat, ornamented with a large silver buckle which caught up the brim at one side. The most splendid article of his attire was his sword-sash, a vivid splash of red and gold against the sober hue of his doublet, from which hung a small-sword. Sash and sword had been a gift from John Ryall, who had seen to it that he had been taught to use the weapon properly.

Settling himself in his seat, he glanced at Deborah, marking the flush of excitement on her cheeks, the bright air of expectancy about her. She sat leaning forward, as though determined to miss nothing, like an eager child. He thought of her admirer of the previous day, and frowned.

At eighteen his sister was on the verge of womanhood. Old enough to be married, to have children of her own. Old enough, and comely enough, to attract the attention – honourable or otherwise – of all and sundry. Comely . . . she was more than that. For a moment he could have wished her plain and pockmarked. No one then would have accorded her a second glance, and he would not have had to worry about her.

As it was, she was his responsibility; his to protect. If only Mattie had come with them! But no; she had declared herself to be too old to go gallivanting. Mistress Deborah would manage well enough – there was sure to be a maid at the inn to lace up her gowns.

His responsibility, but – Philip's face lightened – only until they found their father.

The busy streets were clamorous with the cries of hawkers, and apprentices calling their wares from the shop fronts; with the rumble of iron wheels over cobbles, the frequent altercations between drivers and pedestrians when the latter were bespattered with filth from the kennel by the passing wheels, and also between the drivers themselves when one refused to give way to allow another to pass. Progress was slow and tedious.

"'Twould be as quick to walk," Deborah observed, irked by the constant stoppages.

By this time they had left Fleet Street with its many little lanes and courts behind and, having passed the Temple Bar, entered the Strand. At once Deborah forgot about the traffic and feasted her eyes upon the magnificent houses and the elegant passers-by. It was at once apparent to her that her gown, which had seemed so fine in Hallowden, was completely out of style here.

Her gaze passed from the low-cut bodices and trailing skirts of the ladies, to the short doublets and petticoat breeches of their escorts. She drew Philip's attention to the latter, and he grinned. "Those are the latest fashion. They were brought back by the exiles from Holland. What would you say if *I* were to wear them?"

"Why, that you would look like some strutting barnyard fowl!"

They left the Strand behind, passed Charing Cross, and continued along the road which bordered the Pall Mall alley (where Deborah looked in vain for a sight of the King among those disporting themselves there), and so to St. James's Palace, and Long Street.

Here the driver of their coach brought his horses to a stop, and they alighted. Philip had a short, sharp altercation with him over the fare; saying, as he concluded it and led Deborah away; "The runyon tried to overcharge me. He must have thought I was nothing but a country bumpkin. 'Twas as well I knew the rate was a shilling a mile. Next time I will settle the fare first!"

Deborah nodded somewhat absently, for now they were so near the end of their journey her heart had begun to beat rapidly, and her hand, as she slipped it into Philip's, was suddenly cold with nervousness.

"Here we are, Deb." Philip had brought her to a halt outside a large, imposing house. Long windows faced the street, flanking the heavy oak door. Philip knocked. It seemed to Deborah that an air of brooding silence hung about the place. They had to wait some time before Philip's summons was answered, and the door was opened to them by a young footman in blue livery. He eyed them enquiringly.

"Is Lord Wyngarde at home?" Philip enquired.

The footman shook his head. "No sir. His lordship left for the country this morning."

"Then he's *here*!" Deborah exclaimed excitedly. "I mean – here, in England?"

"Yes, Mistress." The footman thawed visibly before her glowing face.

"So we have just missed seeing him! Oh Philip, if only . . ."

He stopped her with a swift shake of the head, and turned once again to the footman. "How long is his lordship expected to remain out of town?"

"For some ten days at least, sir."

Deborah, unable to contain herself, said quickly, "Has he gone to Wyngarde Court?"

Before the footman could answer, another servant, with the dignified bearing of a butler, appeared on the scene. He sized up the situation with a glance.

"You may go, Martin. I will attend to this."

"They were enquiring for his lordship," the young man murmured.

The butler raised supercilious brows as he took in the plain attire of the two callers, and the fact that they had apparently arrived on foot. His manner became frigid.

"His lordship is away from home."

"Could you. . . ." Philip began.

The door closed.

Philip took Deborah's arm, a spark of anger in his eyes. "Come, Deb. We have at least discovered that our father is alive, and has returned to England. 'Swounds! That fellow will sing a different tune when he learns who we are!"

They retraced their steps along the street, lingering to take a look at the Palace which, during the war, had been used as a prison and barracks. Deborah said gaily: "Let us go and walk in the park now we are here! Oh, *please*, Philip!"

"Very well." He allowed himself to be drawn away, and the anger went from him as they entered the park.

The warm, sunny morning had tempted many people to walk abroad, as they were doing, strolling along beneath the trees; the gallants ogling the pretty young women, and the latter coquetting boldly with them. Deborah, her hand on her brother's arm, was completely unaware of the glances she herself received from those same gallants, but Philip was well aware of them, and his mouth tightened.

"Shall we go back to the inn, Deb? We can take a hackney."

"Oh no!" Her tone was anguished. "It is so pleasant here, and we do not have to return for our dinner until noon."

"Very well." He shrugged resignedly and, seeing she was totally oblivious of the speculative and appraising glances, followed her example and began to enjoy himself.

All at once they saw people gathering a short distance away, beside one of the walks; heard an excited voice exclaim: "The King is coming!"

"The King!" Deborah turned an eager face to Philip. "Oh, couldn't we . . . ?"

"Come, then!"

They hurried in the direction of the growing crowd, hearing as they went the murmur which became a loud buzz of acclaim, as His Majesty approached. With him were several of his courtiers, each vying with the others in splendour and, it seemed, in wit, for there was much talk and laughter, in which the King joined.

Philip and Deborah had reached the edge of the walk when the crowd suddenly surged forward, separating them from each other. Deborah had much ado to retain her balance, and when she was at last able to look about her, she could see no sign of her brother at all. Panic struck her. She was surrounded by strangers, pushing and jostling in order to obtain a better view of their sovereign.

She began to push her way through them, with but one thought in her mind – to find Philip. A hand slid round her waist, and she struck at it blindly and dodged away, hearing a jeering laugh as she did so. She collided with the square figure of a workman in greasy fustian and recoiled from him as he grinned down at her.

Almost in tears, tossed from one side to the other like some small ship upon the surging billows, and by now some distance from the place where she and Philip had come to stand at the edge of the gravelled walk, she felt herself once more thrust against a solid figure. An arm went round her to steady her. A deep, pleasant voice said: "Hold on to me!"

With a gasp she tried to free herself, but at the same moment an elbow dug her in the small of the back and she was flung forward, coming to rest with her face crushed against a broad chest, all the breath knocked out of her.

Trembling, and gasping for breath, she gradually became aware of having found a haven. Her rescuer stood firm, holding her against him until she had recovered sufficiently to lift her head and raise her eyes to his face.

"Thank you!" she breathed.

She found herself gazing up into a pair of dark eyes that searched hers . . . and was unable to look away. There was something in his intent regard, something that leapt like a bright flame between them, that made her feel all at once as though she had never lived before this moment, and nothing would ever be quite the same again.

Her lashes fluttered down upon cheeks suddenly suffused with warm colour. The pulse had begun to beat rapidly and jerkily in her throat. She could not look at him, and yet felt she must.

She stole a quick glance beneath her lashes. He smiled.

"You came to see the King? Then you shall do so!"

His intention was obvious, to force a way through the crowd for her; but she hung back. "Sir! My brother . . . we became separated. He will be searching for me. I must . . ."

"We will find him afterwards, never fear. I saw what happened, and came to offer my assistance to you. Come. . . ."

He began to shoulder his way through the press, his arm round her, holding her fast.

"Make way there! Make way!"

His voice and manner were so authoritative that a passage was immediately made for them. Scarcely knowing how it happened, Deborah found herself upon the edge of the broad walk once more, and there, but a few yards away, was the King. He glanced towards her and, wonder of wonders, smiled!

She felt the pressure of her rescuer's hand upon her shoulder, and as he drew off his beplumed hat and bowed, she sank into a curtsey beside him. The hand was now beneath her elbow, lifting her up, and she raised her eyes to the King's face. His gaze rested upon her and then moved to the young man beside her. He paused in his stride, one eyebrow lifted quizzically, the long mouth curved again.

"My lord. . . ."

"Your Majesty."

With a slight nod and a deepening of that smile, the King passed by.

Deborah gazed after him, everything else forgotten. He had smiled at her! She had read approval, even admiration, in his eyes. She turned a radiant face to her escort.

He smiled down at her. "You have seen the King, and he has seen *you*! – And doubtless envied me."

His voice was soft, his glance a caress. His hand had found hers and was holding it lightly, yet she could feel the strength in his fingers. The crowd milled about them, dispersing now that the King had gone. Excited, gay voices filled the air. People passed, brushing against them. They did not notice. The park might have been empty, for they were aware of no one but each other.

He still held his hat by his side. His thick dark hair was shoulder-length and slightly curled; his face was lean, the features well defined. A handsome face, marred perhaps by a certain cynicism. Deborah did not see it. She saw only the expression in his eyes.

Her gaze fell before it. She looked down at the hand holding hers, half veiled by a fall of lace: a well-shaped hand, well-kept.

Back to her mind came His Majesty's greeting: "My lord. . . ."

With sudden awareness, she took in the details of his appearance – the fashionable short jackanapes coat, diagonally crossed by a fringed sword sash of orange silk, the petticoat breeches adorned with bunches of ribbon loops, the fine holland shirt, the silk cravat edged with lace. His legs were encased in stockings of green silk, heavy silver buckles gleamed on his black shoes.

A courtier. An intimate of the King. Deborah gulped.

"Sir – my lord. . . ." Her voice was stifled. "You have been – so kind."

"Kind?" There was an odd inflection in his voice. He mocked her, then? But no . . . a swift upward glance showed her his face, mouth twisted in a rueful smile that did not reach his eyes. She was conscious of something beyond her understanding, something that left her troubled and perplexed.

And then Philip was beside them, his glance, razor-sharp, flashing from one to the other.

"So *here* you are, Deborah! Whatever happened to you?"

Swiftly she pulled her hand free, launched into a breathless explanation, willing him to understand. Philip was angry. His clipped tones, his lowering look, told her that. She did not realise that his anger masked a growing dismay at finding her in the company of this stranger, this fashionable gallant, as far removed from Deborah's world as a being from another planet. His immediate reaction was to whisk her away as quickly as possible. He scarcely heeded her stumbling explanation.

"—I tried to find you in the crowd, but could not. This gentleman came to my assistance. He has been most – most kind."

"Indeed?" Philip's glance met that of the stranger standing tall and protective by her side. He bowed coldly. "I am indebted to you, sir. And now, pray excuse us. We must be on our way."

The other smiled. "You are in no way indebted to *me*, I assure you! I was only too glad to be of service." He paused, and then added, "Am I right in supposing you are visitors to London?"

"You are." Impatient to move away, Philip ignored the unspoken appeal in Deborah's eyes. "Come, Deb. We are delaying this gentleman."

"Not at all." The man's voice was courteous, his manner friendly; it was as though he chose deliberately to ignore Philip's marked hostility. Bowing to Deborah, he took her hand once more, lifting it to his lips. "Your servant."

She gave him a winsome smile. "Goodbye. . . ."

As in a dream, she allowed Philip to lead her away; and he, managing with some difficulty to contain himself until they were out of earshot, then broke the silence by demanding to know what she thought she was about to allow complete strangers to hold her hand and flirt with her, while half the citizens of London looked on and doubtless drew their own conclusions concerning her virtue.

Face flushed, she rounded on him. "Flirting! Indeed he was not!" How quick she was to fly to his defence! "And as to my *virtue*, I would ask you not to cast aspersions . . ."

"I was only pointing out that others might do so."

"I am not concerned with the opinions of others."

"Then you should be!"

After this exchange, they went on in somewhat strained silence for a while. Then Philip said, making an effort to speak lightly: "Did you see the King?"

"The King?" For a moment she looked blank. "Oh – yes, I saw him. Did you?"

He grimaced. "I was far too intent on finding *you*! No doubt I shall have other opportunities of seeing him."

They paused to allow some people to cross their path. Deborah, noting that Philip's attention was upon them, stole a quick look back over her shoulder. Her rescuer was still there, his figure dwarfed by distance. He had been joined by several other young gallants. Even as she looked, they went off together, sauntering along in easy companionship.

She sighed, and as she and Philip continued on their way, felt suddenly sad at heart. They would probably never meet again. She did not even know his name, save that the King had addressed him as "My lord."

Her lips moved.

"What did you say?" Philip bent his head towards her.

"Oh – nothing." She gave him a little tight smile. "I – I wonder what Mrs. Goffin is preparing for our dinner?"

CHAPTER TWO

WHEN Charles Delaunay, Earl of Mulgarth, rejoined his friends that July morning, he was prepared for their chaffing, turning it aside with good-humoured indifference. No, he had not learned the girl's name, nor had he made an assignation with her. As for her escort – he was her brother.

One of his companions exclaimed, "Ah! Not a jealous husband! Even so, these brothers can be devilish suspicious where their sisters' honour is concerned; eh, George?"

The gentleman appealed to, Lord Aveling, looked momentarily taken aback, but recovering quickly, replied: "Jealous, suspicious – we can all be that. Even a mistress ... especially a mistress!" And amid a chorus of appreciative laughter he added slyly, "Wait until the admirable Mrs. Dennis hears of this morning's encounter. I'll warrant she'll not be best pleased to learn another has taken your fancy, Charles!"

Charles eyed him levelly. "Don't be a fool, George. 'Twas a chance meeting, nothing more. I am not likely to set eyes on the girl again. James, are you coming my way?"

Sir James Leveson, whom Charles had known since boyhood, was as fair as he was dark. The two friends, having taken their leave of the others, made their way out of the park. Glancing at Charles's face, James said tentatively, "George will have himself run through one of these days, with his careless tongue."

"Not *careless*, James. It was said deliberately, in order to distract my attention from Harry's words, which I suppose we all understood."

James looked uncomfortable. "I wasn't sure whether you knew—"

"About George and my sister Helen? Oh yes, rumours *have* reached my ears, though I must confess I have so far ignored them in the hope that having nothing to feed upon, they would die a natural death. It seems I was wrong."

"I don't think the attachment has become serious yet, but you know George's reputation. If Helen were *my* sister, I'd take good care to keep her away from him. Indeed, I had intended to speak to you on the matter. She is, after all, barely twenty; and even though she *was* married, it wasn't a real marriage . . ."

"Wedded, but never bedded," murmured Charles, "for which circumstance she may count herself fortunate, having regard to the character of my late brother-in-law. I gather you are trying to tell me it is time I took a hand in the affair."

"You *could* send her down to Hertfordshire to stay with your grandfather. When I think of her with that – that libertine, it's as much as I can do not to run him through myself!"

"Odso! You'd best calm down, my friend. It's far too hot for violence!"

James gave a wry smile. "You know how fond I am of her. 'Tis no secret between us. I'd have offered for her long before this, had I thought I stood a chance. Indeed, I was beginning to have hopes . . . and then George stepped in, plague take him!"

"Don't despair!" said Charles lightly. "Once George is out of the way, your turn will come."

"I hope so!" James fell silent for a moment, then he said, "Will you be seeing Lydia Dennis today?"

Charles gave him a quick look. "Yes, probably. Why do you ask?"

"I was recalling George's words, and wondering whether some distorted version of this morning's incident might reach her ears." James spoke carefully, aware of treading on dangerous ground. "You don't think she might come to the wrong conclusion?"

"She may choose to believe it or not, as she wishes." Charles's tone was perfunctory. Clearly he had no intention of discussing his mistress, and James was left to wonder whether the scraps of gossip he had recently heard about them were true: that they had quarrelled and were on the verge of parting.

The lady in question was young and beautiful, the widow of a Royalist who had died in exile. Charles had met her in Brussels, and brought her back with him when he had returned to England in the spring, from his own self-imposed exile. James guessed that his friend was by no means the first to have become Lydia Dennis's lover. Not that he thought any the less of her for that; rather did he pity her. To be young and beautiful and widowed, and above all, penniless ... life could not have been easy for her.

Since their return, Charles had installed her in a pleasant house in the neighbourhood of Covent Garden. She lacked for nothing; and yet, it seemed, had chosen to quarrel with him. Could it be that love had died between them so soon?

Having promised to take dinner with his uncle, a gentleman of some wealth to whom he stood as heir, James left Charles at the corner of Drury Lane. The latter sauntered home alone, pausing now and then to speak to acquaintances, though he was in no mood to linger, being preoccupied with his thoughts.

Arriving at his house, a fine Palladian mansion in Great Queen Street, he found a note awaiting him from Lydia. He broke the seal and scanned it quickly: a few carelessly written lines expressing her regret that she would, alas, be unable to keep her appointment with him that evening, as she had unfortunately succumbed to a chill. Perhaps, in a day or two. . . .

Tearing the sheet across, Charles tossed the pieces aside, and flung his hat and gloves after them, a servant stooping quickly to retrieve them.

By the time the man had straightened again, his master had crossed the hall to the book-room, the windows of which faced on to the garden at the back of the house. He seated himself at the big walnut table on which stood a silver standish containing ink and goosefeather quills, paper, and two neatly arranged piles of newsheets and pamphlets, which had obviously been tidied by the maidservants when they had cleaned the room that morning.

Taking a quill, freshly cut for him and ready for use, he tried the tip of it on his finger, dipped it in the ink and then sat staring into space.

"Deborah. . . ." he whispered.

He and his friends had been watching with some amusement the way the people were rushing to catch a glimpse of the King. It was always the same: it seemed that wherever he went, King Charles was surrounded by wildly-acclaiming multitudes. Restoration fever, some called it. The King basked in the heat of it, with his lazy, cynical smile, listening with never-failing courtesy and patience to the host of petitioners clamouring for posts and privileges, many of which were granted with a generosity which was, perhaps, part of that same Restoration fever; disarming his subjects with the warmth and humour of his personality.

All over England they drank his health and rejoiced that he had come into his own at last; and if he was not as they expected a King to be – so different in every way from that aloof monarch, his father – they loved him all the more because of it.

Watching the crowd that morning, Charles's attention had been caught by the two young people who had come to stand at the edge of the walk, only to be engulfed by the sudden surge of the throng which had thrust them apart. Aveling had found it amusing; he had not. He had caught a glimpse of the girl looking wildly about her; had known, even at that distance, that she was frightened and, on impulse, had gone to her rescue.

It had been easy enough to find her, for he was taller than most, and well able to push his way through the milling mass. A movement of the crowd had sent her into his arms, and when at last she had recovered her breath and lifted her eyes to his, he had found himself looking into the sweetest face he had ever seen; a heart-shaped face framed by that glorious golden hair. He could still feel the wonder of that moment;

his absurd, insane desire to sweep her up in his arms and carry her away to some haven where there would be just the two of them. . . .

He could see her now, in his mind's eye, gazing up at him. Her eyes, he recalled, were blue-grey, long-lashed, her nose tip-tilted, her chin dimpled. And her mouth . . . her mouth was made for laughter. And for kisses.

All his inclinations had been to further their chance acquaintance. He knew his friends had expected him to do so. None of *them* would have let such an opportunity slip by, with the possible exception of James. Even the presence of her brother would not have daunted them.

He could not help wondering whether she would have been averse to his advances. She was very young – inexperienced and naïve compared with the women he had come to know. Was that, then, why he had been so attracted to her? – Because she was different, because she had about her an air of innocence?

He suddenly found that he had driven the point of his quill into the sheet of paper before him. He stared at it, without really seeing it; then threw it down, his expression dark and bitter.

She had thanked him for his kindness. . . . *He*, whose associates for the past four years had been libertines and demireps, who had learned to live with vice and intrigue and turn a blind eye to both, who had whiled away the hours in drinking and dicing because there was nothing else to do, except fall into bed with a willing wench . . . *any* wench.

He had left England after quarrelling with his father over his sister Helen's marriage to Lord Revett, a man many years her senior, whom Charles had despised and hated because of his licentiousness. The Earl had insisted upon the match, pointing out its advantages: Revett was worth thousands, with estates that brought him a considerable revenue. Helen's future would be secure.

As it happened, the marriage had never been consummated, for the bride, being then too young to be bedded, had returned to the parental fold; while the groom, continuing on his dissolute course, had succeeded in drinking himself to death before the year was out. It was almost as though the Earl had had some strange foreknowledge of the turn of events.

Charles had never seen his father again. He had died suddenly, leaving Helen in the care of their grandfather, the Marquis of Welford, while Charles had been abroad.

He thought of the boy he had once been; with all a boy's idealism. A boy as innocent as the child he had rescued today – plunging willy-nilly into the vortex of life at the King's Court in exile; returning to England a man, hardened and cynical. He had no illusions any more, certainly none about himself. Yet he suddenly found that it hurt to admit that there was seemingly little difference between him and those among whom he had lived for the past four years, who now formed the pleasure-loving, back-biting, self-seeking element at Whitehall.

The King, though he might not be the worst among them, was certainly far from the best. With his example before their eyes, it had been all too easy for his fellow-exiles to succumb to the temptations that had in time left their marks upon blotched and ravaged countenances. He thought of the King, who was thirty and looked ten years older; of Buckingham, whose handsome vitality was already coarsening as a result of his excesses.

And himself? He was twenty-five, and could thank God and a strong constitution – and perhaps an innate good sense, that had kept him from indulging in those very excesses that had destroyed Revett and were threatening to send Buckingham on the same path – that he looked no more than his age, and enjoyed excellent health.

His thoughts returned inevitably to Deborah. How could he forget her? Yet forget her he must, for her own sake, if not for his. She was not for him, with her sweet face and artless simplicity.

And yet. . . . He recalled again that sudden heart-stopping moment when she had looked up into his eyes, and all at once he knew the truth. He had fallen in love with her – deeply, irrevocably in love.

He pictured her in this house, her presence warm and endearing. Here, by right; not to be kept as a mistress in the background of his life, but as his wife, to share that life with him. Yet, how could it be? As Earl of Mulgarth he would be expected to marry someone of noble birth, who could bring him an adequate marriage portion. Someone of whom his grandfather, the redoubtable Marquis, would approve. Charles made a wry grimace. He feared the Marquis would most certainly *not* approve of his grandson marrying a girl chance-met, however bewitching she might be.

With a deep sigh, he drew another sheet of paper towards him, took a fresh quill and dipped it in the ink. After a moment's thought, he began to write.

For Philip and Deborah the next few days were filled with sight-seeing. Philip had decided that having assured themselves their father was alive and back in England, they might now enjoy a holiday while they awaited his return to London.

He had already written to Mrs. Crabbe, the housekeeper at Hallowden Grange and the only person there who was able to read and write properly. How pleased Mattie and Luke would be to hear the good news!

Having visited London before, Philip felt he knew enough about it to be capable of conducting Deborah to the places she had set her heart upon seeing. After their first few days he suggested that in order to conserve their funds, it would be best for them to travel on foot, instead of taking hackney coaches. Deborah agreed wholeheartedly. Her experience of hackney travel, with its many long and tedious hold-ups in the congested streets, had not endeared itself to her. There was, besides, so much to see that everything was a source of great interest to her.

Philip, strolling by her side, smiled at her evident enjoyment, thankful that she appeared to have forgotten her encounter in St. James's Park. In this supposition, however, he was mistaken. Always at the back of her mind was the thought that she might meet her gallant rescuer again, at any moment – at Whitehall, perhaps, or in Hyde Park, or in any of the other places to which Philip took her. But the days slipped by, and there was no sign of him.

They visited the Tower, and listened to the mountebanks in Tower Street; mingled with the crowd on London Bridge, where Philip lingered at the little bookshops and Deborah at the haberdashers, and both came away the poorer in pocket: he with a copy of Ben Jonson's *Bartholomew Fair*, she with a small, painted chicken-skin fan. Philip, saying he would give her the fan as a present, reimbursed her, and later, when they visited the Exchange in Cornhill, added a pair of perfumed leather gloves.

The next morning found them in Hyde Park. The day was hot and the streets airless; the stench rising from the kennels and manure-heaps even more noisome than usual. It was refreshing to wander over the grass, where they found a seat on a bench in a welcome patch of shade. Deborah had brought her fan and Philip, taking it from her, fanned her cheeks with it, in the manner of the young blades with their ladies.

All at once he paused, head turned, then stood up, thrusting the fan into Deborah's hand.

"Listen, Deb! It sounds like a horse bolting! Yes . . . here it comes!"

A black horse, eyes rolling, mouth foaming, galloped wildly across the grass, people scattering before it with shouts and screams. For a moment Deborah sat there, staring; then, with a gasp of alarm, sprang to her feet.

She caught a swift glimpse of the rider, striving desperately to remain in the saddle – a young woman, dark hair streaming, face white.

She heard Philip shout at her to get out of the way. Instinctively she obeyed him, expecting him to follow suit. Instead, to her horror, he leapt forward, caught hold of the bridle, and hung on. Hands pressed to her mouth to check the scream that rose in her throat, Deborah watched helplessly as he was dragged along, stumbling and slipping over the grass.

Gradually, however, the horse's reckless pace slackened. He began to respond to the pressure on the bridle, and finally came to a halt, sides heaving, flecks of foam on his sweating coat.

Philip, as exhausted as he, took several steadying breaths before raising his head and looking up at the rider. She was leaning limply towards him. Her hair brushed his cheek and her eyes, still shadowed with fear, looked into his.

She put a hand on his shoulder. Her mouth quivered. "You were – wonderful!"

He was about to disclaim the tribute when, with a little moan, she swayed and fell. He just managed to catch her in his arms, staggering beneath her sudden weight.

A crowd of people had gathered round them by this time, with an excited buzz, marvelling aloud at the young man's bravery. Philip, concerned only for his fair burden, scarcely heard the plaudits. Deborah, having salvaged his hat from beneath their feet, found herself quite unable to get near him, standing on tiptoe in an effort to see what was happening.

Another rider came up: a gentleman in elegant riding dress, who flung himself off his horse, threw the bridle to his groom, and swept purposefully through the crowd.

"Helen, my dear!" he exclaimed; and then to Philip, "I cannot thank you enough for your brave action, sir! Some damned dog ran under the horse's feet, and startled him."

The girl had opened her eyes at the sound of his voice. She glanced up into Philip's face, a faint smile on her lips.

"You may . . . put me down now, sir."

He set her gently on her feet and she remained there, leaning against him, head resting on his shoulder. He supported her as best he could with the people jostling round them until her escort took charge of the situation.

"Give her air, please! Here – let me. . . ." Without warning, he took the girl from Philip and swung her up in his arms, the crowd parting as he strode away to a group of trees nearby. Laying her down on the grass, he fell on to one knee beside her, chafing her hands in his, and murmuring in rallying tones to her. She had recovered somewhat by this time and Philip, who had followed after them, was thankful to see a tinge of colour in her cheeks. She saw him watching her, and smiled again.

"I shall never forget your bravery . . ."

He was suddenly aware of his disordered appearance: shoes scraped, stockings, with tags loosened, wrinkled about his legs, one shoulder seam burst open and his shirt plainly visible through the gap. He passed a hand over his hair in a swift attempt at tidying it, conscious – only too conscious – of a pair of blue eyes studying him with some interest beneath thick black lashes.

Her hair was a dark cloud about her face. She looked no older than Deborah at that moment, though he guessed her age to be nearer his own. The man beside her was several years her senior, handsome enough, but with an air of dissipation about him that Philip was quick to detect.

His manner with the girl was distinctly possessive. He smoothed the hair back from her forehead, remaining on one knee, his arm supporting her, until she had fully recovered. He then assisted her to her feet, remaining close beside her, his arm about her slender shoulders.

He thanked Philip once more for his courageous action, his manner courteous, but nevertheless with a note of dismissal in his tone. It was evident to Philip that he was expected to bow gracefully and depart. A muscle tightened in his cheek. So be it! As he straightened from his bow, however, he found a slender hand held out to detain him, heard a soft voice say in some distress, "I fear you have torn your doublet, sir! I had not realised . . ."

He glanced swiftly down at himself, and shrugged. "'Tis nothing, I assure you. It can be mended easily enough."

Her gaze on his face, the girl moved a step forward, away from the arm that encircled her shoulders. Her companion, with a slight frown, beckoned the groom over to them and the latter came up with the horses.

"I do not think we have met before, sir?" There was a question in her tone.

"No," Philip replied. "I have not been long in London."

"Indeed? You are staying here for a while?"

"For a while." He hesitated, uncertain how to explain his affairs to her. Had they been alone, he felt he could have confided everything to her, for already he was conscious of a growing awareness between them that might have developed into something deeper. But he could not do so with her escort standing within earshot and tapping his whip impatiently against his boot, now that she showed every sign of wishing to linger.

"Come, my sweet." The gentleman was waiting to lift her into the saddle.

"Goodbye, sir." The girl smiled up at Philip, her hand once again extended to him. He took it, and bowed, brushing it with his lips.

"Your servant."

He remained standing there as they moved away, watching them, the trace of a smile on his lips, expression abstracted. He came out of his reverie to find Deborah at his elbow, her anxious gaze fixed on his face.

"Deb!" He had completely forgotten her.

She handed him his hat, exclaimed over his appearance, and began to brush him down in an attempt to remove the dust from his garments. He stopped her irritably. His one desire now was to return to the Gilded Peacock to assuage his thirst and relax his aching limbs.

They soon found a hackney, and as they were borne away from the park, Philip sat back with a sigh of relief, scarcely troubling to answer Deborah's questions, for he felt disinclined for conversation. After a while he became aware that she too had lapsed into silence, and was sitting beside him, looking down at the fan in her hands with an odd concentration, her lips drawn tight.

"Deb—" He touched her hand. "I'm sorry. I didn't intend to be sharp with you."

"It doesn't matter." She looked up at him, her eyes suspiciously bright, and then burst out, "Oh, Philip! I thought you would be *killed*!"

The tears brimmed over and began to trickle down her

cheeks. He slipped an arm about her. "Silly little goose!" he said affectionately. "Here, take this."

He gave her his kerchief. She mopped up the tears, blew her nose, and managed a watery smile.

"She was very beautiful, wasn't she? Did you learn who she was?"

"No." His voice was low. "Only that her name was Helen."

The next day being Sunday, they went to church, Philip electing to attend St. Bride's in Fleet Street.

His doublet had been mended, and his shoes restored to some semblance of their former glory by the boot-boy's ministrations. When Deborah had anxiously enquired this morning whether he felt any the worse for his exploit, he had replied somewhat shortly that he had never felt better, apart from a certain soreness in the palms of his hands, as a result of gripping the bridle so tightly when he had been dragged along. Deborah thought he looked heavy-eyed, as though he had not slept very well, but refrained from commenting upon it, sensing that he did not wish to be drawn upon the matter.

Indeed, Philip had found sleep elusive. Over and over again he had relived every second of the dramatic episode in the park, especially with regard to the young woman whose life he had saved. He remembered every little thing about her: the dark cloud of hair, the perfect oval face with its clear blue eyes, patrician nose, lovely red mouth and fine skin; her long, slender hands, the sweet fragrance which had enveloped her. She had been tall and well-shaped, with an air of delicate refinement. A young goddess. . . .

His thoughts had turned to her companion. He had not been her husband; was she, perhaps, betrothed to him? There could, of course, be another relationship between them, but Philip's mind baulked at it. He did not want to think of them . . . of *her* . . . sharing such a relationship.

Not unexpectedly, his attention wandered sadly during the service, and he heard no more than the first few sentences of the sermon, although Deborah commented favourably upon it afterwards.

They walked sedately back to the inn for their dinner, turning their backs upon the evil-smelling Fleet Ditch and the Bridewell Prison. A playbill fastened to the sooty trunk of a plane tree caught Philip's eye, and he drew Deborah's attention to it. Perhaps she would care to pay a visit to the playhouse one afternoon?

She turned excitedly to him. Could they really go? Would he take her to a playhouse – that den of vice and wickedness that all the Puritans thundered against so loudly?

"Why not?" he said, smiling broadly at the expression of surprised delight on her face.

Neither of them had been inside one. They had never had the chance. The playhouses had been closed at the beginning of the Civil War, and had only recently been re-opened, after eighteen long years. Deborah, brought up during the Interregnum, when all forms of entertainment had been forbidden as licentious and sinful, could still not quite bring herself to believe that she was not breaking all the laws of God and man by entering such a place. In fact, though she did not know it, William Davenant had been producing plays there during the years of the Commonwealth, in defiance of the law, and at the risk of prosecution.

The next afternoon, however, decked out in her blue taffeta and carrying her fan, she hurried along beside Philip to the Cockpit Theatre in Drury Lane, where they found themselves drawn along in a merry throng of all classes of people, from gay blades of the Court to servants and apprentices.

Philip hesitated momentarily between the choice of seating and then, in rash mood, slapped down eight shillings for admittance to a box near the stage. Deborah gasped at the cost, but he said airily that they might as well make the most of their first visit to a play, and whisked her inside.

The playhouse was filling rapidly with the noisy audience, and was already disagreeably hot and stuffy when Philip and Deborah entered their box. Having settled themselves, they looked about them with great interest. Deborah feasted her eyes on the elaborate gowns of the ladies, several of whom, she noticed, carried vizard masks. Perhaps, then, it was still considered not quite proper to attend a play?

She had little time to speculate upon it, for her attention was caught by the entry of a number of gaily-clad young gentlemen who, judging by their voluble high spirits, had indulged themselves exceeding well at the dinner-table. With much horseplay and ribaldry, they finally took their seats on the benches in the pit, from which vantage point they proceeded to comment freely and at length upon all and sundry, from the Court gallants and their bejewelled mistresses, to the pretty orange-sellers who moved between the benches, selling their fruit at sixpence apiece, and returning the comments of the young bloods with a coarse and ready wit.

Deborah shrank back when their bold glances discovered her, sitting beside Philip. One of them actually rose from his seat and bowed in would-be dignified fashion to her, blowing her a kiss, before he was pulled down again by his companions.

Philip's brow darkened. "Unmannerly lowns! I am beginning to think this was a mistake."

"Oh no!" She was at once perturbed, fearing that he might take her out again, and they would miss the play. "They will be quiet when the performance begins."

The play, *The Loyal Subject*, was due to start at three o'clock, and the audience was growing noisily impatient by the time a boy with a taper came on to the platform stage, and proceeded to light the row of candles across the front of it.

This was greeted by a cheer from the bright sparks in the pit, followed by another when, shortly afterwards, an actor in gay costume and curled wig appeared and, when the noise had quietened, bowed this way and that, and recited the prologue.

Deborah's gaze was fixed on the stage from that moment forth. She sat a little forward in her seat, hands tightly clasped round the ivory holder of her fan, cheeks flushed, eyes shining, her whole attention riveted upon the performance, determined not to miss a single word of it.

In the first interval she turned to Philip. "Isn't it splendid? Are you enjoying it?"

"Very much." But his tone was somewhat abstracted, and he brought his gaze to her face as though with an effort, from a close study of one of the boxes on the opposite side of the playhouse. Then, with a sudden brightness, he smiled and took her fan.

"Allow me." He fanned her hot cheeks, engaging her in conversation until the play recommenced.

When it did so, and Deborah had fixed her attention once more upon the stage, he felt free to resume his study of the occupants of that other box; or, to be more exact, of *one* of them, and she well repaid his scrutiny. Her hair, that dark cloud he remembered so well, was dressed in becoming and fashionable style, caught up at the back and with side ringlets falling to her bare shoulders. Round her neck was a heavy pearl necklace, and pearl pendants hung from her ears.

Her gown, low-cut, was of shimmering pale green silk, the sleeves opened down the arm, caught together here and there with pearls. Her face did not glow as Deborah's did, for it had been carefully painted with ceruse, and her cheeks and mouth reddened with Spanish paper.

For a brief moment he remembered her as he had first seen her in Hyde Park, hair loose and flowing, riding dress disordered, leaning against him, limp and defenceless. She was far less approachable now, with her magnificent jewels and fine gown, elaborate coiffure and fashionable toilette. Everything about her spoke of a way of life far above that which he and Deborah had known at Hallowden.

Tearing his gaze from her he fixed it upon the stage, trying to concentrate upon the action of the play; but in a little while his eyes returned to her once more. This time he spared a glance for her escort, and as he had expected, found it was the gentleman who had been riding with her. He was clad in oyster satin, a fine cravat at the neck, a froth of lace at the wrist; leaning towards her and evidently whispering in her ear, for she raised her fan in front of her face and laughed, shaking her head so that the pendant ear-rings swayed.

They were in a party that occupied two adjacent boxes, and had arrived just as the play had begun. Philip had only noticed them towards the end of the first act; his eyes immediately lighting upon the young woman's face to the exclusion of all else. And now the joy of seeing her was tempered by the painful knowledge that their worlds were poles apart.

And yet – were they? A feeling of excitement stirred within him. He had forgotten his father, forgotten that, within a few days' time he would be returning to London. From that moment their whole lives – his and Deborah's – would be completely changed.

He, Philip, would no longer be a young man with no prospects, but the accepted heir to Wyngarde, and all it entailed. The house might have fallen into decay, but it could be restored – rebuilt, if necessary. The revenues from the estate would once more be paid into the Wyngarde coffers. There was the fine house in Long Street. His father could petition the King – might already have done so – for some remuneration for all he had lost. . . .

All manner of fanciful notions entered Philip's head. He saw himself, the man of fashion, in rich attire, strolling through the Stone Gallery at Whitehall, with the lovely Helen on his arm. . . . And then smiled wrily to himself. Dreams were one thing, but the reality was not so easily attainable.

CHAPTER THREE

AT the end of the play, Deborah applauded enthusiastically and then, with a tremendous sigh, turned to Philip.

"How wonderful it was! I do hope we can come to the playhouse again, if Father will permit it."

"We must wait and see."

Philip was hustling her out of the box with what seemed to her to be inordinate haste, but she supposed he was in a hurry to return to the inn for his supper. She gave one last backward look round the emptying playhouse as though to stamp it for ever on her memory – the now bare, darkened platform stage round which, on three sides, the audience had sat; the pit, strewn with litter; the two rows of boxes. Older, more world-weary eyes might have seen its tawdriness, the dirt beneath the veneer. To her, the whole afternoon had been touched with magic. She was reluctant to return to reality; but Philip's hand was beneath her arm and he was leading her out.

His first thought when the play ended was to leave as quickly as possible, for, when his glance had returned to Helen and had then strayed to the rest of the party, he had received a disagreeable shock. In the other box, seated beside an attractive fair-haired woman in rose-pink, was the gentleman who had come to Deborah's aid in St. James's Park. He had been gazing at Deborah with the same fixed concentration as that which he, Philip, had turned upon Helen.

A quick glance at his sister's face had shown Philip that she was totally unaware of it, and indeed remained so for the rest of the performance. So far as he was concerned, this was all to the good. He did not want Deborah to be confronted by her knight errant. He also found himself strangely reluctant to meet Helen with her elegant escort. It would be far better for Deborah and himself to slip away unnoticed.

His intention was admirable; unfortunately it was thwarted. When they had entered the playhouse, the sun had been shining, but now, to their dismay, they found that rain was falling steadily.

Philip glanced at Deborah. She had left her cloak at the inn, not wishing to be burdened with it at the playhouse. He could not expect her to walk to Holborn through the rain.

"Stay here, in the shelter of this doorway," he said quickly. "I will go and find a carriage. Don't move!"

He hastened away, and was soon lost to her sight in the crowd.

The street was filled with the waiting coaches of the gentry. One by one they collected their owners and were driven slowly and ponderously away over the uneven cobblestones. The less fortunate hunched their shoulders and hurried away to their homes, or to some welcoming tavern.

Others, in no particular hurry to leave, stood about in groups, seemingly indifferent to the rain. Among these were the noisy young blades who had invaded the pit. They were now arguing as to where they should go for supper, contrasting the merits of the Falcon in the Paris Garden with those of the Devil at Temple Bar.

One of them – the one who had bowed to Deborah before the commencement of the performance – caught sight of her and advanced towards her with purposeful air and weaving gait. She eyed his approach with some trepidation and looked anxiously round to see if, by lucky chance, Philip was returning; but there was no sign of him. She turned away, hoping that if she ignored him, the fellow would leave her alone. He did not.

Coming to a halt beside her, he doffed his hat and bowed with exaggerated courtesy.

"Sweet young lady, nymph of delight, ad-adored one, do not t-turn your back upon one who would kneel at your – at your little feet. . . ."

Deborah, who had stiffened at the first words of this preposterous address, now found to her startled surprise that he had seized her hand and conveyed it to his lips.

"Don't do that!" She snatched it from him, cheeks burning, eyes flashing.

"Ah, don't be angry! Just one smile from those sweet lips . . . one limpid glance from those bright eyes . . . 'tis all I c-crave from you!"

He swayed towards her and, to steady himself, placed a hand upon the wall beside her head, leaning against her, his face hanging over hers. She shrank back as far as possible into the doorway, her indignation rapidly giving way to growing panic. It was a situation without precedence for her. She had not the slightest notion how to handle it. Had she had any idea of Philip's whereabouts, she would have dodged past this pot-valiant jackanapes and taken to her heels. As it was, she could only hope that Philip would return, or that someone would come to her aid. And, at that moment, someone did.

"Sir, you are annoying this young lady. I suggest you return immediately to your friends!"

That voice! She looked up, eyes widening. "My lord!"

It was indeed he who had come to her rescue, sending her tormentor purposefully about his business with a strong hand on the back of his neck and a push that propelled him into the midst of his fellows, who received him with a gust of derisive laughter.

Charles turned back to Deborah. She was gazing up at him, her expression one of mingled gladness and relief.

"Oh, sir! – My lord! Thank you. . . ."

He smiled. "We did not exchange names when we met before. Allow me to introduce myself – Charles Delaunay, Lord Mulgarth, at your service."

"I am Deborah Ryall." She spoke the name without thought; for so many years she had used it.

He uncovered and bowed. "My duty, Mistress Deborah." He looked about him. "Surely your brother has not abandoned you in such a cavalier fashion?"

"Indeed no! He has gone in search of a carriage."

Her voice was a trifle breathless. She was deeply aware of his nearness, his polished manner and air of self-assurance. She felt uncertain and at a loss, conscious of her simple gown and plain toilette, in such direct contrast with the rich elegance of his own attire. Raising her eyes to his face she found him gazing intently at her. The colour rose in her cheeks.

Hesitantly she said: "Did you enjoy the play?"

"Very much. And you?"

"Oh yes! I had never been to a playhouse before."

"Then it was a new experience for you."

"Yes. We were in a box."

"I know."

"You saw us there?" She looked startled. "I did not see *you*."

A smile touched his lips. "You were concentrating upon the performance. I must confess my own interest in it dwindled considerably from the moment I became aware of your presence."

She gave him an uncertain look. "You said you had enjoyed the play, but if you were not watching it . . ."

He took possession of her hand. "I should have said, I enjoyed the afternoon."

He kissed her fingers one by one, his gaze holding hers; knowing full well that despite her valiant attempt to appear indifferent to him and to treat him lightly, she was fast becoming entangled in her emotions. Her hand trembled in his.

Experienced enough to know the effect he was having upon her, Charles was suddenly smitten with contrition. He had resolved that she was not for him; that, should their paths cross again, he would make no attempt to pursue her. Yet, here he was, laying siege to her heart with soft words and kindling glances – the opening salvoes which had led to many a conquest in the past, when love had been but a game to him.

But now . . . now it was no longer a game, and she was not

just another conquest. She was someone special, set apart from all the others.

His hand had tightened involuntarily round Deborah's, his expression darkening with the intensity of his thoughts. He became aware of her own expression – uncertain, bewildered by the change in him.

He smiled, and her face lit up.

"How very sweet you are!"

The words, spoken in low tones, seemed to hover in the air between them. Had he really spoken them aloud? He supposed he must have done, for her eyes were shining like stars as she gazed up into his face. Once again he felt that wild, wonderful urge to sweep her up in his arms and carry her away.

And then, without warning, Philip came up to them. Neither had noticed his approach. With a hostile glance at Charles, he greeted him with a marked lack of warmth, and to Deborah said that there was not a carriage to be had, but he had managed to find a chair for her. The men were waiting. She had best come at once.

Deborah detained him, with a hasty explanation as to the reason for his lordship's presence by her side. Philip thanked him stiffly, impatient to lead his sister away.

"Have you far to go?" Charles enquired.

"To the Gilded Peacock, in Holborn," replied Deborah.

Philip frowned. He had been too late to check her; he had not wished to inform his lordship of their address. The latter was saying he would have been only too happy to place his own coach at their disposal, had he not had some friends with him.

"I thank you for the kind thought," said Philip smoothly. "Come, Deb. Lord Mulgarth will wish to return to his friends."

His lordship, however, seemed to be in no hurry to do so. He accompanied them to the chair, and was about to hand Deborah into it when the fair-haired beauty Philip had seen with him in the playhouse moved towards them. Her glance raked Deborah from head to foot, taking in every detail of her appearance, before she turned to Charles. Deborah had the impression that she had been dismissed as being of no importance.

"My dear Charles, we were wondering where you had disappeared to!" The lady's voice was languid and drawling. She stood there, a cloak of violet silk over the rose-pink gown, the hood drawn over her head. Her attitude was imperious, slightly impatient; her smile did not quite reach her eyes.

"I apologise for keeping you waiting." His lordship's tone was curt. "Why do you not sit in the coach with the others? I will be with you in a moment."

Deborah saw the lady's mouth harden, a spark of anger in the long green eyes. With a petulant shrug she turned, saying, as she began to walk away, "Please don't be too long, Charles! You know how my cook dislikes to be kept waiting."

His lordship did not reply. Deborah, glancing quickly up at him, found that his expression was dark, his mouth drawn tight. He looked down at her, and she smiled apologetically.

"I am sorry. I am keeping you standing here in the rain."

Handing her into the chair, he bowed over her hand. "Adieu, Mistress Deborah. Mr. Ryall." With a smile to them both, he turned and strode away.

Deborah barely had time to see him climb into a heavy, gilded town coach with four horses to draw it, before the chairmen lifted her chair and began to bear her away. She sat back and allowed herself to pretend that she was seated in that coach, beside *him* . . . just the two of them, going back to supper together. An intimate supper, with wine and beautifully cooked delicacies, waited upon by discreet footmen. . . .

Philip's face appeared, framed in the window. "Are you comfortable, Deb?"

The vision faded. She blinked, and assured him hastily that she was.

He smiled and straightened, and walked along beside the chair, scarcely heeding the rain or the puddles that lay before his feet, deep in thought.

When he had left Deborah sheltering in the doorway, he had gone at once to find a carriage, weaving his way through the throng of playgoers that swelled about the entrance to the Cockpit, not really taking much note of them until, at a sudden touch on his arm, he had checked to find himself looking into Helen's face.

"Why, sir! How came you here? Were you at the play?"

She had been wearing a cloak and hood of burnt orange over the misty green of her gown, the rich colour glowing in the dull light beneath the heavy grey sky.

Philip, uncovering, had bowed to her and to Lord Aveling, the latter acknowledging his greeting with the barest lift of the lips before his gaze roved among the press of people once more, searching for acquaintances.

"I came with my sister. I have left her sheltering from the rain while I look for a carriage."

"A carriage? George—" She had turned impetuously to her escort. "Could you not send Browning for one?"

Lord Aveling, frowning momentarily, had conceded that he supposed he could, and had despatched his servant forthwith upon the errand. He had then been hailed by friends, and for a few minutes – immeasurably precious to Philip – had left them alone together.

Looking back now to those few minutes, Philip tried to recall every word that had passed between them. They had discussed the play, the weather, the crowd, and then she had said, "I fear I did not thank you properly for saving my life. At the time I was so distraught, I did not even enquire your name. My own is Helen Revett."

"Philip – er – Ryall." He had hesitated over the surname, but if she had noticed it, she made no comment; and then the servant had returned with the information that there was not a carriage to be had, but he had obtained a chair for him. Philip had thanked him, slipping a coin into his hand.

He should have returned to Deborah then and there, but still he had lingered by Helen's side, unwilling to tear himself away from her. And then Lord Aveling had returned, and

Philip, perforce, had had to go; only to find, when he had rejoined his sister, that she was no longer alone.

Once again his first reaction had been one of alarm, especially when he had noticed the way in which she and her companion had been gazing at each other, lost to the world, it seemed. He recalled her explanation that she had been accosted by one of the rowdy fellows who had invaded the pit that afternoon, and that his lordship had come to her assistance. Very commendable of him, but it had not given him the right to hold her hand in such a blatant fashion, and to look at her as though. . . .

"I must speak to her!" he resolved.

His interview with Deborah, which occurred in the small private parlour directly they returned to the inn, took a slightly different course to that which he had anticipated. Instead of listening meekly to his admonition, she became heated and flew to the defence of Lord Mulgarth, declaring that Philip did not understand, and was being grossly unfair. His lordship had treated her with the greatest kindness and respect. If he, Philip, had not deserted her for so long, there would have been no need for someone else to have to protect her from the unwanted advances of others.

Philip, uneasily conscious of the truth of this last statement, nevertheless maintained that Lord Mulgarth's manner had been far too familiar, adding that if she were not so bemused by him, she would acknowledge the fact herself.

"That's not true!" Deborah had cried, and before he could check her, had whirled out of the parlour and rushed away to her bedchamber.

After this, of course, the atmosphere between them was somewhat strained. Having partaken of her supper in almost complete silence, Deborah announced her intention of going to bed early, and with a swift peck on Philip's cheek instead of her usual goodnight hug and kiss, she left him.

Philip sat on for a while, brooding upon the vagaries of young women until, with a shake of the shoulders, he got up and went outside. The rain had ceased, though it still dripped from the eaves and ran gurgling along the gutters. He decided to go out and seek some amusement. Just because Deborah had gone to bed with the sulks, there was no cause for *him* to do so. And after all, he had not been out alone since they had come to London, apart from visiting the nearby barber's shop each morning for a shave.

He went up to his bedchamber for his hat, and then hesitated momentarily outside Deborah's door, but hearing no sound from within, decided not to bother to knock and tell her of his intention. Instead he passed on, descended the stairs, and went out into the street.

All London lay before him. Soon it would be candle-lighting time, the streets and alleys and squares full of shadows, vague and mysterious; when sounds of revelry would issue forth from the open doorways of inns and taverns; when a silken petticoat would swish against one's legs, a whiff of perfume invade one's nostrils, a pair of eyes smile invitingly.

But he did not want that kind of company, Philip decided. Not tonight, when Helen filled his thoughts to the exclusion of all others. Lost in those thoughts he wandered along, oblivious to his surroundings until he was brought swiftly back to awareness of them by the approaching rumble of a coach and four, and had to skip smartly out of the way, cannoning into a passer-by.

"Careful, dunderhead!" the man exclaimed furiously. "Can you not look where you are going?"

Philip began to apologise, and then his words trailed away as recognition dawned. It was none other than Deborah's admirer from the stage-coach. The latter recognised him in the same instant. Immediately his manner changed to one of affability.

"My dear fellow! Who would have thought . . . well, well!" He beamed upon Philip, enquired after Deborah, and then insisted that Philip should accompany him to a "cosy little tavern" in Fleet Street where, he said, he was joining some friends in a private room.

"No, no!" he exclaimed, when Philip demurred. "I insist

upon it! You will enjoy it there; good company, good wine. Come, sir! The night is yet young."

Somewhat unwillingly, Philip allowed himself to be borne away, and was presently following his companion, who had introduced himself as Edward Osborne, into the Mitre tavern where, as the evening progressed, and the waiter brought in measure after measure of sack and syllabub, together with such delicacies as anchovies and neats' tongues, he began to view everything in a different light. Osborne was the best of good fellows, London the finest city in the world, the Mitre the veriest gem of a tavern, and the company the most convivial a man could wish for.

Having joined them in the singing of ballads and catches, he had then been drawn into a game of ombre for moderate stakes . . . and then another, and another. So the evening passed, and the room became hotter, the candlelight blurred, the cards danced before Philip's eyes; and he lost again. He pushed the money across the table.

Another game? – No, no. It was late. He must get back to the inn. He got to his feet, swayed, clutched at the table and promptly sat down again. His head was swimming. He closed his eyes for a second. . . .

Someone was shaking him. Curse the fellow! Why couldn't he leave him alone?

"Wake up, Ryall! Wake up!"

He groaned, and opening one eye, found he was lying half over the table, head pillowed on his outstretched arms. With an effort, he raised himself, blinking. Osborne was beside him, the others preparing to depart.

"'Tis gone twelve, my dear sir." Osborne seemed little the worse for the night's carousing. He was probably used to it.

"Mus' go back to the inn," murmured Philip.

"Of course. . . . Unless you'd rather go somewhere else first? I know of a very good address, not far from here." Osborne's tone had dropped to a confidential murmur. "Kept by a most discreet woman – friend of mine, in a manner of speaking. She'd be only too happy to accommodate you with one of her girls – charming little misses, all of 'em. None of your common punks there! What d'ye say?"

Philip groped for his hat. "No, I'd sooner not. But you – don't let me keep you from . . ."

"I'll see you on your way – stranger to London – can't have you losing yourself. Too many crackropes about."

The night air was cool, with a moisture-laden wind blowing from the river. Philip lifted his face thankfully to it. His head ached, his eyes were heavy, his legs decidedly unsteady. Had Osborne not been with him, he would not have had the least notion which direction he should take. As it was, they had not gone more than a short distance before an empty carriage came along and Osborne hailed it. He set Philip down outside the Gilded Peacock.

"Here you are, Ryall. Tell Mistress Deborah I will pay my respects to her tomorrow – Er, that is to say, *today*!"

The coach rattled away, doubtless bound for Osborne's "very good address", and Philip turned to go into the inn. As he did so, he heard a furtive movement behind him. He swung round, almost losing his balance in the process, and his hand brushed against something . . . *someone*. A man. Quite a small man, though it was too dark to see him properly. Agile, too. Before Philip could do more than clutch at a rough frieze coat, he had twisted free and backed away out of reach, poised for flight.

At that moment, the inn door opened. A shaft of light illuminated the scene. For an instant, the man's face was clearly defined: a thin face, sharp-featured beneath a battered old hat decorated with a broken feather. Just for an instant; then he was gone, bolting down the street like a rabbit for cover. The darkness swallowed him up.

"Did he prog your purse, sir?" It was the tapster, at Philip's elbow.

"My – purse?" Philip looked at him stupidly, then gathering his befogged senses, groped in his pocket. "No, it's still there."

"You were lucky then, sir. The town's full of padders and

pickpockets, always ready to take advantage of a gentleman who's – er – been enjoying himself." He took Philip's arm and led him over to the doorway. "Come along, sir, I'll take you up to your room. 'Tis time you was abed."

CHAPTER FOUR

HE still had his purse... but the evening's play had lightened it considerably.

Philip emptied it on to his toilet table and grimaced. Rapid calculation showed that he had enough to pay Mrs. Goffin for their second week's lodging (he had already settled the reckoning for the first); but there would be little left after that.

What a fool he had been! Osborne and his friends could well afford to lose their money at cards. *He* could not. If he had had any sense, he would have left earlier in the evening, instead of sitting there like a pigeon waiting to be plucked.

This morning his head ached abominably, and there was a foul taste in his mouth. He picked up his small hand-mirror and stared dejectedly at his pallid reflection.

A knock at the door heralded the appearance of Deborah. Hastily, he swept the money back into his purse and pocketed it before bidding her enter. She came in, giving him a measuring look.

"I trust you enjoyed yourself last night," she said distantly. "Might I ask where you went?"

"To the Mitre in Fleet Street, with one of your admirers!"

Her eyes widened. "One of my – ?" The colour came and went in her cheeks.

He surveyed her sardonically. "Oh, not his *lordship*! He would scarcely deign to spend an evening in a tavern! No, it was the gentleman we encountered on the stagecoach. I bumped into him – literally – and could not shake the fellow off. He insisted that I should join him and his friends for a convivial evening...." No need to tell her about the money.

"His name, by the way, is Edward Osborne, and he intends to pay his respects to you, some time today."

"Does he?" There was a marked lack of enthusiasm in her tone.

"I gather the prospect does not exactly please you. I would suggest that the only way to avoid him is to be out when he calls."

"Oh yes! Where shall we go?"

He recollected the state of his finances. "We could visit Long Street again to see if Father has returned. Didn't that footman say he should be back within ten days?"

Deborah agreeing to this with some alacrity, they set out on foot directly after breakfast. There was a bubble of excitement within her, for who could tell – at any moment they might meet Lord Mulgarth!

Upon reaching Long Street, Philip went straight to the house and banged peremptorily upon the door, although the place bore the same silent air as before. The haughty butler answered the summons, his brows rising as he recognised them. He informed Philip disdainfully that Lord Wyngarde was not at home, and closed the door forthwith.

"Scurvy runyon!" Philip said forcefully, and then shrugged. "Ah well! I should have guessed Father had not returned, for the house is still shut up."

He began to stride away, with Deborah hastening by his side. "We will come again tomorrow," he decided, "and the day after, and the day after *that*, until he returns; but we will not trouble ourselves to enquire. We shall know by the look of the place whether Father has returned or not."

Having turned their backs upon Long Street, they walked along to the great sprawling mass of buildings which comprised the palace of Whitehall. They had already, on another occasion, visited the Stone Gallery, in which members of the public were allowed to wander freely; so this morning, as Philip's head was still aching, they elected to remain outside in the pleasant gardens.

Finding a stone bench set in a shaded alcove, they sat there for a while, watching the crowds of sightseers, exalted and humble alike, passing by. Philip then suggested that instead of walking back to the inn through the hot, clamorous streets, they should take a boat as far as the Temple Stairs. It would not be so far to walk from there.

The boats, rowed by stalwart oarsmen, were moving continually up and down the river, carrying passengers from one set of stairs to another, for a few pence. Philip and Deborah made their way to the slippery steps at the river's edge, and found a boat waiting, having just discharged its passengers. The two oarsmen were clad in somewhat soiled and sweaty shirts and doublets, with old Monmouth caps on their tousled heads. Philip cast a doubtful look at them, but Deborah, having been helped aboard and settled comfortably on the cushions in the stern, turned a dazzling smile upon them, receiving a broad grin from each in turn.

"Oh, this is splendid!" she exclaimed, as the men, plying their oars skilfully, took the boat away from the bank and out into the stream.

Philip, sitting beside her with the river breeze cooling his aching brow, was inclined to agree.

Whitehall slid away from them. Deborah, gazing at the many windows of the palace which faced the sparkling water, wondered aloud whether the King might be standing at one of them. Perhaps she ought to wave her kerchief?

One of the boatmen informed her with a grin that she would be wasting her time if she did so, His Majesty having sailed down river in his state barge at an early hour to look over a Dutch pleasure-boat, called a "yaugh", or some such outlandish foreign name, which the Dutchies had sent him as a gift, and which was now moored below London Bridge.

"He was up before you, mistress, I'll warrant!" he said. "There's no keeping *him* in his bed these fine mornings."

"No," the other put in quickly, "and from what *I've* heard, he's not above sharing it! Body o' me – there's many a drab will find her way advanced by climbing the Privy Stairs and serving His Majesty! They do say he had mistresses aplenty in them foreign parts he was in, and one came back with him, a Mrs. Palmer. I saw her once – a real beauty!" He smacked his lips and winked at Deborah, who stared at him, round-eyed, a trifle disconcerted by this gratuitous piece of information.

They left Whitehall and its Privy Stairs behind, and continued downstream past the mansions of the Strand, with their gardens sloping down to the water's edge, coming at last to the Temple Stairs.

Here they disembarked, and having settled with the men, went up the steps, through the quiet, shaded Temple gardens, and so back to the inn, where the first person they saw was the very one they had hoped to avoid . . . Mr. Osborne.

He came towards them, smiling, and having uncovered, greeted Philip, and bowed over Deborah's hand. How well she looked! He trusted she was enjoying her stay in London, and would not think it amiss of him for waiting upon them.

"Of course not," Deborah murmured, gently withdrawing her hand from his clasp. She glanced obliquely at Philip. "My brother has told me of the pleasant evening he spent in your company. How fortunate that you should meet each other."

"Fortunate indeed!" breathed Mr. Osborne, gazing into her eyes. "Tell me – what have you seen of London, so far?"

"Has not Philip told you? The Palace at Whitehall, the Tower, Westminster Abbey. . . ." Deborah proceeded to tick them off on her fingers.

Philip stood a little apart, racking his brains to try and think of some excuse to be rid of Osborne. It seemed obvious that he had sought them out with the intention of attaching himself to them, at least for dinner, if not for the rest of the day. And who, Philip asked himself bitterly, will be the one to defray expenses?

He was right so far as dinner was concerned. It now being the hour at which the meal was served at the inn, he could scarcely turn the man away, however unwilling he might be to request the pleasure of his company. Osborne accepted his invitation with ready enthusiasm. He proceeded to eat heartily of all that was put before him, setting himself out to entertain them with a fund of anecdotes and, as the meal progressed, to embark upon a mild flirtation with Deborah beneath her brother's watchful eye.

Deborah, aware of Philip's disapproval, took a certain delight in encouraging their guest. Outwardly all beguiling innocence, inwardly she was filled with mirth. At the end of the meal, Osborne wiped his lips with his napkin, and turned to Philip, wishing to know whether he had made any plans for what was left of the day.

"If you have not," he said, "may I suggest something which I think will please you both?" He smiled at Deborah. "How would it suit you to take a basket of provisions up-river to Chelsea, in a sailing boat, or if you would prefer, down to Greenwich? There is nothing more delightful than a river trip, I assure you! A fine, warm evening, pleasant company, plenty to look at as we drift along, a good supply of food and drink, and returning home when the sun is setting and the first stars shining in the sky!"

"I don't think. . . ." Philip began.

"Oh, come – don't refuse me! You will enjoy it, and so will Mistress Deborah, I'm sure. Why, she has already mentioned how much she liked the short river trip you both took this morning. I'll tell you what, sir: I know a most charming young woman who would be only too happy to make up the party. There – what do you say?"

He glanced hopefully from Deborah's bright face to Philip's frowning one. The latter still hesitated, not wishing to commit himself, since the convivial Mr. Osborne had not made it clear who was to foot the bill. The gentleman's next words, however, relieved him of that doubt.

"I shall be only too happy if you will consider yourselves my guests for the evening," he declared.

Philip glanced enquiringly at Deborah.

"It sounds very pleasant," she said.

Osborne beamed. "Then that's settled!"

Settled it was, and Philip had not the heart to refuse, though he did not look forward with any pleasurable expectancy towards the evening spent in the company of Osborne and his friend.

This proved to be a young woman by the name of Althea, with voluptuous figure and languid manner, whose glossy curls caressed plump white shoulders. Philip could not help but wonder whether she was one of the "charming little misses" Osborne had previously recommended to him. As the evening progressed, and they partook of the provisions in Osborne's basket, she gradually lost her languid air and became quite playful and kittenish toward Philip, offering him titbits which he was expected to eat from her fingers, and nestling cosily against him in a most beguiling – not to say intimate – manner.

Occupied with parrying her advances, Philip had little time to observe Osborne's attentiveness towards Deborah, which by this time had become very marked indeed. She discovered that it was one thing to conduct a mild flirtation with him beneath her brother's vigilant gaze; it was quite another to have to cope with him more or less on her own.

The two boatmen took no notice of them, apparently used to turning a blind eye to the behaviour of their passengers.

Sitting as far away from Osborne as possible, Deborah found that he had moved nearer and placed an arm round her shoulders. She wriggled and glared at him but he took not the slightest notice. Instead, he gazed soulfully into her eyes and began to pour a stream of flowery compliments and honeyed phrases into her unwilling ear, his hand straying beneath the curls that rested against her neck

She turned her head away, frowning down into the dark water. They were returning through the summer dusk, through the soft, warm air. She suppressed a sigh. How enchanting it would have been had someone else been sitting close beside her. . . .

She was trailing her hand in the water, and all at once something slimy and clinging floated into it. She bit back a sharp exclamation, glanced down, and saw that it was the remains of a cabbage in an advanced state of decomposition. A gleam of mischief came into her eyes. Osborne, emboldened by her quiescent air, leaned even further towards her, his breath on her cheek.

"So sweet a flower," he breathed ardently. "So . . . eh, what!"

Without warning, Deborah shrieked. She brought up her hand, still holding the rotting vegetable, and with another shriek, let it fall into Osborne's lap. For a moment he stared with stupefaction at the soggy mass and then, with a violent shudder, flung it overboard. Deborah, all apologies, seemed to be on the verge of tears at her unfortunate action. She turned hastily from him, kerchief pressed over her mouth, shoulders shaking, while he tried frantically to mop his soaking breeches and efface from them the odour of decaying cabbage.

Shaking she was, but with suppressed laughter. It was not until they had taken their leave of Mr. Osborne and Althea that she was able to allow her mirth full rein, laughing until the tears ran down her cheeks.

Philip, recalling Osborne's astounded face, laughed too. Nevertheless, he resolved to avoid him in future, not only because of his own dwindling resources, but because he viewed with some alarm that gentleman's determined advances to Deborah. Osborne had mentioned making up a party to visit the Mulberry Gardens one evening . . . music, wine, delicacies to tempt the palate, secluded arbours. . . .

"I'll see him hanged first!" Philip declared to himself.

His fears were allayed, temporarily at least, by the arrival of a note from Osborne next day, to the effect that he had been called out of town on business, but hoped to wait upon them on his return to London.

For the next few days Philip and Deborah made their way to Long Street every morning, but without success. The house retained its silent, closed-up appearance.

Every evening, Philip would turn out the contents of his purse and frown over the result. The end of their second week was looming nearer. Mrs. Goffin would be wanting to know if they wished to keep the rooms on for yet another week, and would most likely expect him to settle the amount they owed her for this present one. He still could not bring himself to tell Deborah the truth: that, owing to his own foolishness, they would have little money left when they had settled the reckoning.

Meanwhile, his chief concern was to keep expenses to a mimimum. If Deborah wondered why they walked everywhere, why he discouraged her from looking in the shops or lingering in the street markets, and seemed disinterested in her tentative suggestions for river trips and other outings, she said nothing, although she gave him a slightly puzzled look at times.

And then one morning, as they rounded the corner into Long Street, Deborah stopped and clutched at Philip's arm. Outside their father's house stood two magnificent coaches.

"He's back!" she cried excitedly.

"Calm yourself, Deb!" But Philip was excited as she, despite his attempts to appear unruffled. He grinned down at her. "This time that portly runyon *will* have to admit us!"

As it happened, the butler requested them to wait while he ascertained whether his master was at home. It seemed to Deborah that he left them for an inordinately long time before returning. He then requested them to follow him, leading the way towards a room at one side of the hall, from which came the buzz of conversation. Evidently Lord Wyngarde was entertaining company.

"Whom shall I announce?" enquired the butler.

"There is no need for you to announce us," Philip said swiftly. "We will introduce ourselves to his lordship."

The butler, looking dubious, pushed open the double doors, and ushered them inside.

"The – *callers*, my lord!" He withdrew, closing the doors behind him.

It was a large and spacious withdrawing-room, its windows overlooking the street; with another room opening off it, a glimpse of which could be seen through a partly open door. Deborah's first impression was that the withdrawing-room was full, her second, that the company was exclusively masculine. The hum of conversation died abruptly as she and Philip hesitated just inside the doorway. All eyes were turned upon them in frank curiosity.

Feeling at a distinct disadvantage beneath this scrutiny, Deborah moved closer to Philip; and then, across the room, her gaze met that of someone she knew . . . Lord Mulgarth. Her heart gave a little leap. He was staring at her with an expression of startled surprise, as though he could not quite believe his eyes. She smiled. He would be even more surprised when he learned the reason for their visit!

Philip had already recognised Deborah's knight-errant, and also another gentleman, Lord Aveling; giving each a curt nod. Mulgarth, he saw, was preparing to come over to them. Aveling merely raised an eyebrow, and turning to his companion, said something in a swift undertone which was received with a sniggering laugh.

Philip's mouth tightened. If this was the company his father kept . . . ! But where *was* his father? None of those present seemed to be much over the age of thirty.

"Sir?"

A gentleman had approached them; clad in the height of fashion, dark hair carefully curled, grey eyes holding an expression of keen interest. His nose was slightly acquiline, his mouth firm and well-shaped, but thin. His manner was courteous, his smile warm and encouraging, deepening when he looked at Deborah. Everything about him was agreeable; yet for some unaccountable reason Philip distrusted him, sensing perhaps that beneath his charming manner lay a will of steel, a formidable, relentless determination that would stop at nothing in order to achieve his purpose.

"Lud, the fellow's lost his tongue," said a mocking voice.

Philip flushed, and bowed stiffly to the man before him. "I beg your pardon. I wish to see Lord Wyngarde."

The well-marked brows rose slightly. "You *are* seeing him, sir."

Philip stared at him. "I don't understand. . . ."

"*I* am Lord Wyngarde."

"But –" Philip tried to collect his scattered wits. "Sir – I think there must be some mistake."

The rest of the room had been listening with great interest. Now came a guffaw from a red-haired young gentleman brandishing a wine-glass.

" 'Sblood! He's calling you a liar to your face, Howard!"

Philip found Lord Mulgarth at his side. "There is no mistake, sir," Charles said quietly. "I can assure you this gentleman is the person you wish to see."

Deborah stared from one to the other in growing bewilderment. "But – but he *can't* be! Lord Wyngarde is our father!"

There was a moment's stunned silence, broken by another guffaw from the red-haired gentleman, who had now helped himself to some more wine. One of his fellows demanded of his host whether he could supply them with the details of such an amazing phenomenon, for he must, he added, have fathered them at an extremely early age.

Philip's jaw hardened. "Sir, you may scoff as much as you like! Lord Wyngarde *is* our father. I do not know how this gentleman came to take the title."

Charles eyed him narrowly. "In the natural course of events, Mr. Ryall. He inherited it."

"*Inherited* it!" Philip's gaze returned to the man before him, in mute enquiry.

The other shrugged. "Allow me to clarify the position for you. The late Baron was my uncle. Perhaps you are unaware that he died in Brussels, nearly two years ago? I was with him at that time, and as my father had already died, I inherited the title." He paused, surveying Philip coolly, then continued, "Perhaps you are also unaware that it is generally known that his two children died during the war." There was an undercurrent of menace in the measured tones.

Philip ignored it. "You are Francis Wyngarde's son?"

The other bowed. "And *you*, sir?"

"My name is Philip Wyngarde. This is my sister, Deborah."

"Indeed? I was under the impression that my friend, Lord Mulgarth, addressed you a moment ago as 'Mr. Ryall'."

Philip made a swift movement, aware of Mulgarth's searching glance. "Yes, he did. It is the name we have used since the day we had to flee from our home. Our cousin, John Ryall, took us in, and subsequently brought us up. It was thought safer for us to conceal our true identity from the world."

"You are asserting, then, that *I* am your cousin?"

"Yes." Philip glanced at the others, all listening avidly; at Mulgarth regarding him beneath drawn brows. "Perhaps it would be better if we could discuss this matter in private."

"I have nothing to hide from my friends. Pray continue, Mr. – ah – Wyngarde."

"The matter is a little delicate. You mentioned the fact that we – my sister and I – were supposed to have died during the war. That story was put about at the time of our father's escape and our mother's death. It was done to save us from whatever fate *your* father intended for us." He eyed Howard Wyngarde thoughtfully. "If, as you say, you were with my father in Brussels, I presume you were not in agreement with Colonel Wyngarde's policy?"

"No, sir. I have always been sympathetic to the Royalist cause. I left England voluntarily to live in Flanders rather than remain beneath the yoke of a Government which was entirely abhorrent to me."

His words brought a loud burst of approval from his friends.

Philip's eyes narrowed. "So you went to Flanders and joined my father?"

"I joined Lord Wyngarde . . . yes."

"It never occurred to you that you might not be the rightful heir? You made no attempt to verify the story of our deaths?"

For a brief moment Howard hesitated, then he laughed contemptuously. "My dear sir! Enough of this play-acting! Do you seriously expect me to swallow your cock-and-bull tale? You must take me for a complete gaby!"

"Sir!" Philip drew himself up, eyes flashing dangerously.

Howard's glance flicked over him. "I will allow that you and your sister *may* be the children of the late Baron Wyngarde, my uncle, but to put it bluntly, on which side of the blanket were you born?"

"What!" Philip's hand went to his sword.

Deborah gasped, and caught at his arm. "No, Philip! Don't!"

Howard smiled. "You would be wise to take your sister's advice. . . ."

"Ecod, yes!" This from a gentleman in wine-red doublet and full petticoat breeches, who proceeded to inform Philip that their host was one of the most accomplished swordsmen in England, and he had better think twice before challenging him to a duel. There was a buzz of agreement, Aveling remarking that such a meeting might teach the insolent young upstart a lesson he sorely deserved.

Philip flashed a smouldering glance at him.

Howard said: "It is obvious to me that you became acquainted with the tale of the Baron and the unfortunate deaths of his two young children, and decided to come to London with the intention of passing yourselves off as his heirs. Unfortunately for you, your scheme has misfired. I would strongly advise you to return forthwith to whatever rustic retreat you came from, before I hand you over to the law. Incidentally . . ." his expression became sardonic ". . . my butler informed me, before admitting you, that you have been haunting the house for the past fortnight. Kindly refrain from doing so in future. I shall give orders for my servants to report to me if you so much as set foot in the street."

"Are you threatening me?" demanded Philip.

"Merely safeguarding myself. I have no desire to meet with – shall we say – a fatal accident."

Philip stiffened, but before he could speak, Charles said in clipped tones, "Have you any means of substantiating your claim, Mr. Wyngarde? Documentary proof, for instance?"

"Documentary proof," Philip repeated slowly; and then, "Yes, I believe I have." His expression cleared. He turned swiftly to Deborah. "When Mother sent us to Cousin John, she gave Luke some papers to take to him – you remember? He showed them to me once. . . ."

Charles looked at Howard Wyngarde. "Well, Howard? I suggest you leave matters as they are for the moment, until Mr. Wyngarde can produce his evidence."

Howard smiled thinly. "Very well." His gaze returned to Philip. "When you have found your documents, bring them to me. I shall be extremely interested to see them." His tone was laden with sarcasm.

"You will, of course, wish to submit them to your lawyers," Charles murmured, and Howard glanced at him with a slight flicker of annoyance.

"Of course." He nodded to Philip. "I await your pleasure, Mr. Wyngarde. – Terris!" He raised his voice, and the butler appeared immediately from the hall. "Show the two visitors out, and then come back at once. I wish to have a word with you."

The butler bowed majestically. Philip took Deborah's arm and led her out, barely acknowledging Howard's polite "Good day!", and giving her time for only a fleeting glance at Lord Mulgarth. But that glance was enough to show her his aloof expression; and her heart sank. If *he* did not believe Philip's story, then things were black indeed!

From the room behind them came a sudden burst of conversation. Clear above all else they heard the words, " 'Twas as good as a play, I declare! 'Od's truth! I've never met with a more audacious rogue!"

Another voice broke in: "I thought at first he had come to offer you his sister, Howard. To be sure, 'twould not have been such a bad idea! She's a bewitching little armful, if one's taste runs to sweet innocence."

"First come, first served." Lord Aveling's mocking tones were easily recognisable. "Mulgarth has prior claim upon her. . . ."

" 'Sdeath!' Philip whirled about, hand once more on his sword hilt. "Leave me alone, Deb! The fellow shall not get away with it!"

"No, no!" she begged, almost in tears. "Please, Philip – let us go from here!"

He looked down into her flushed, pleading face. "As you wish."

With a glance at the butler's imperturbable countenance, he stalked out and, once in the street, gave vent to his feelings in an explosive outburst; ending – "So much for your gallant admirer! He's no better than the rest! *'Prior claim'*, indeed!"

He marched Deborah away and she went blindly, her throat choked with tears. His lordship wasn't like that . . . he couldn't be! And though the others might mock and pour scorn and derision upon Philip and herself, surely he believed in them? Nevertheless, she could not easily forget the shadow of doubt in his eyes and her heart was heavy.

After a while, she managed to compose herself. "What are we going to do now?"

Philip's reply was prompt. "We will return to Hallowden, of course. When I have found the papers I'll come back to London, and *then* see what our dear cousin has to say! For I'll tell you this, Deborah – I'll not rest until I have made him eat his words! We suffered enough at his father's hands; and now, to find that *he* has usurped the title – !"

She sighed. "And our father dead . . ."

His hand tightened round hers. "We still have each other, Deb."

She nodded, albeit soberly. The day that had begun so well now seemed clouded; the future no longer beckoned. Supposing Philip could not find the papers? What if Cousin John had inadvertently destroyed them? They would then have nothing to support their claim. They would be branded as impostors, held in contempt for the rest of their lives.

The world would be dark indeed.

CHAPTER FIVE

No sooner had his guests taken their departure than Howard strode over to the door leading into the other room and thrust it wide open. His gaze fell upon the man who was sitting within, at a table littered with documents and letters; a man who, at the sight of him, gave a nervous start and rose hurriedly to his feet: a man Philip and Deborah would have recognised at once as Edward Osborne.

Howard said peremptorily, "Come in here! I've something to say to you!"

"Yes, my lord." Osborne dropped the quill he had been holding, the ink on which had long since dried, and hastened after Howard, who rounded upon him with the words:

"You heard? You saw them?"

Osborne gulped and nodded.

"Well, what have you to say for yourself? You led me to believe they were dead; that the story was true." Howard's expression was murderous. Osborne flinched visibly. "What the devil do you think I pay you for? I sent you to Hertfordshire to find out the truth. . . ."

"My lord, as I told you, I made the most extensive enquiries. Everywhere I went, I heard the same thing – that the late Baron's children had died of a fever years ago. I – I enquired not only in Wyngarde Cross, but in all the surrounding villages as well. . . ."

"And had not the wit to search further afield! I might have known you would bungle the whole business! They'll be off to fetch those confounded documents as soon as they can hire some transport. I've told Terris to send Judd to follow them and report back to me when he has discovered where they are lodging in London, but if he proves to be as blockheaded as *you*...."

"I – I can tell you where they are lodging."

"*You* can tell me?" Howard stared at him. "How did you find that out?"

Osborne moistened his lips. "I chanced to meet them..."

"Where was this?"

Osborne hesitated momentarily, then blurted out: "On the stagecoach, travelling to London. I ... my lord, I swear it never occurred to me that they could be the ones you were seeking!"

He broke off with a sudden gasp as Howard, taking firm hold of the front of his doublet, pulled him towards him and, eyes black with fury, proceeded to inform him in the strongest terms exactly what he thought of him. He then released him with a violence that sent him staggering back against a heavy elbow chair.

"And now tell me the truth before I wring it out of you! You met them on the stagecoach; and then—?"

Haltingly, Osborne told his story. Howard listening with close attention.

"The Gilded Peacock," he murmured slowly, and turning away went over to a side table and poured himself some wine. As he drank it, Osborne took the opportunity to straighten his dishevelled garments, watching him uneasily the while.

"If they travelled on the stagecoach," Howard mused, "they will doubtless return in the same manner, which means they will have to go to the coach-office to procure seats." He stood there for a moment, deep in thought, then nodded with an air of grim satisfaction. "I'll have another word with Terris."

"You – you would not seek to – to harm them? Mistress Deborah...."

Howard turned a look of sardonic amusement upon him. "She attracts you, does she? I thought she might. Tell me, have there been any other meetings?"

Flushing beneath his stinging tone, Osborne mumbled

that he had arranged a river trip for Mistress Deborah and her brother.

"How enterprising of you! I presume this was while I was away? What a pity I sent for you to join me before you could ripen your acquaintance with so delectable a nymph!" Howard set down his glass with a sharp movement; then, with a complete change of tone, said abruptly, "I have no intention of harming *her*. Does that set your mind at rest? And now, get out, and send Terris to me!"

Philip and Deborah had little appetite for their dinner. Neither of them had much to say, preoccupied as they were with troubled thoughts. At length, however, Philip said tentatively: "I shall have to settle the reckoning with Mrs. Goffin and tell her we are leaving."

"Yes." Deborah looked up from her trencher. Something in her brother's expression made her ask swiftly what ailed him.

He gave her a wry smile. "What would you say if I were to tell you I have barely enough to cover the reckoning?" He plunged forthwith into an explanation, finishing with the words: "I should have confided in you before, but I could not bring myself to admit what a fool I had been!"

"Poor Philip! I knew *something* was worrying you, but had not the least notion what it could be. 'Tis fortunate I have some money left – enough, I hope, to cover the cost of the coach tickets."

After the meal they set off on foot for Aldersgate Street, Deborah having handed the contents of her purse to Philip. The sky had become overcast, in keeping, thought Deborah, with their spirits. She found herself recalling what had happened that morning, and then, with an effort, put it from her mind.

She looked about her. As always, there was much to see. Coaches, chairs, tradesmen's carts, the little shops with their overhanging upper storeys, the people in the streets, some hurrying about their business, others dawdling along. Beggars ran after the coaches, whining for alms, hawkers called their wares. Here a ballad-monger broke into a snatch of song, there a crippled man dragged himself along on an improvised crutch, wheezing out a tale of gallant service to the Crown in the war, to all who cared to lend an ear.

He followed at their heels until Philip resignedly tossed him a penny, and then, with a "God bless you, kind sir!" hobbled away, much to Deborah's relief, for the smell that had risen from his tattered attire had been decidedly unpleasant.

It was shortly after this incident that they took the wrong turning, and found themselves in Cheapside. Here they became caught up in a noisy, vociferous crowd surging around the pillory and pelting its hapless victim with rotten vegetables. Deborah's sympathies were roused, but Philip led her away before she could give expression to them.

"Do you want the crowd to turn on *you*? Come, we still have quite a way to go, and I don't want to be late back for supper." He cast an eye at the lowering clouds. "We shall soon have rain. 'Twas as well you brought your cloak. I . . . oh!"

Someone had jostled against him, almost causing him to lose his balance. He turned quickly, in time to see a small, thin man making off in the opposite direction.

"Clumsy oaf!" he exclaimed wrathfully.

They reached Aldersgate Street as the first drops of rain began to fall. Philip slipped a hand into his pocket, and then stopped dead. Deborah came to a halt beside him, looking up into his face, which had suddenly lost colour. His expression was one of growing stupefaction.

"Deb! My purse . . . it's gone!"

"Oh no! Surely not! You had it a short while ago, when you gave alms to that vagrant."

"We have come some distance since then, and were delayed by the crowd round the pillory. . . ." His voice died away. His eyes narrowed. "Deborah! That man . . . the one who pushed against me! I'll wager he picked my pocket! It never occurred to me at the time. I wish I had caught a glimpse of his face."

"*I* did. 'Twas long and thin, with a crooked nose, and – and I think he had a broken feather in his hat."

"A broken feather? Now where . . . of course!" he snapped his fingers. "He tried to pick my pocket once before, outside the inn, on the night I met Osborne. We must try and find him!"

They hurriedly retraced their steps. The crowd still milled about the pillory, despite the rain. Philip began his search, asking here and there whether anyone could tell him the whereabouts of a small thin man, wearing a shabby frieze coat and a hat with a broken feather. No one could, or if they could, did not choose to do so.

Finally, he had to admit defeat. "'Tis no use, Deb. We had best go back to the inn."

"You could report the matter to the local constable."

"I doubt whether he would be of much help. He would probably say it was my own fault for not guarding my purse better."

Disconsolately, they returned to the Gilded Peacock and over their supper discussed the situation.

"We could sell something," Deborah suggested tentatively, mopping up gravy with a piece of bread and then letting it lie there, untasted.

Philip frowned. "Sell what?"

"There's my pearl brooch – the one that was Mama's. It would fetch a few pounds, surely?"

"No." Philip's tone was decisive. "It is entirely my fault that we are in these straits. If we must sell anything, it will be something of mine." He paused, considering, and then added, "I could sell my sword. . . ."

"Oh no!" Deborah knew how much he prized it. She cast about in her mind for some other way of raising the money they needed. "Perhaps we could borrow from someone?"

"Borrow from whom? Who do we know well enough in London who might be willing to advance us the money?"

"Mr. Osborne," she replied promptly.

He grimaced. "Yes . . . if we knew where to find him. As far as we know he is still out of town."

"Perhaps he has returned."

"We still do not know his address."

"They may know it at the Mitre. We could enquire there."

"'We'? If there's any enquiring to be done, *I* shall be the one to do it."

"But, Philip. . . ." She put her head on one side, demurely beguiling. "Don't you think he might be more inclined to help us if *I* were to ask him? He does seem to entertain a certain fondness for me. . . ."

He gave her a resigned look. "Oh, very well! We'll go along to the Mitre this evening."

It was still raining a little when they went out, and the sky was already darkening. There were plenty of people about, and quite a number of coaches and chairs, conveying their occupants for the most part towards the well-to-do quarters of St. James's, Westminster or the Strand. Some of them were probably bound for Whitehall, Deborah thought; and she tried to imagine what it would be like to attend a reception there, her expression suddenly wistful.

Neither she nor Philip noticed the two figures following them, slouching along, hands thrust deep into the pockets of their greatcoats, hats pulled well down over their faces. Burly figures these, with little to say to each other, but who seemed to have an unspoken understanding between them, for when Philip and Deborah came at last to the Mitre and went inside, they separated – one going in, the other waiting in a convenient doorway.

Philip led Deborah into the candlelit common-room, where a scurrying potboy loaded with pewter ale-cans paused for a moment to inform them that the landlord had just taken some refreshment upstairs to a private room, but if they cared to wait . . .

They found a vacant settle and sat down, Deborah loosening the strings of her cloak and pushing back the hood. She looked about her with the greatest interest, never having been in such a place before.

The room was full, the air thick with pipe smoke and the accumulated smells of cheese, onions and pickles, ale and wine and unwashed humanity. There was an atmosphere of conviviality and cheer; men played at cards or backgammon, discussed the affairs of the day, laughed and joked together, argued and disputed; drank deeply, waxing mellow or quarrelsome according to their nature.

Deborah noted that the company, though predominantly masculine, yet contained a sprinkling of the fair sex. Instinct told her what kind of woman would frequent a place like this, and would behave in so bold and provocative a manner.

One of them, with a sallow, painted face framed with black ringlets, went to join a man who had just entered. They sat down near the door, their heads close together, deep in conversation. As Deborah watched, the woman suddenly turned her head and stared at her across the room; a keen, speculative glance that Deborah found disconcerting.

The landlord bustled up to them, smiling and jovial. He recognised Philip at once, but on being told the purpose of their visit, shook his head regretfully. Oh yes, he knew Mr. Osborne well enough, but had not the least notion of his address. As far as he knew, he was still out of town.

Philip thanked him, and after bidding them both a civil "Good evening", he excused himself and hurried away to serve some customers.

Philip looked at Deborah, a wry smile on his lips. "It seems I'll have to part with my sword, after all!"

It was still raining when they left the Mitre. Deborah paused to pull her hood over her head and, hugging her cloak about her, set off beside Philip at a brisk pace along the street, both anxious to get back to the Gilded Peacock as soon as possible.

With night fast approaching, there were fewer people about. Occasionally a coach went by, spattering them with muddy water. The streets were so narrow that, when two vehicles passed each other, there was little room left for pedestrians, who had to keep as close to the wall as they could. Candlelight shone from the windows of houses and taverns, but this only seemed to intensify the patches of shadow between. The wind had risen, setting all the signs creaking and swaying, and blowing the rain into their faces.

They turned into a narrow lane, a short cut between two wider thoroughfares, where stood some old, timber-framed houses. In the daytime it was gloomy enough, but at this hour, it was doubly uninviting.

Deborah was just beginning to wish they had not entered it when all at once there came a rush of footsteps behind them. Philip swung round, uttered a sharp exclamation and, thrusting her swiftly behind him, went to draw his sword.

Even as he did so, however, the two men were upon them, whipping short, heavy cudgels from the deep pockets of their greatcoats. Before Philip had a chance to defend himself, he was struck a savage blow on the head and another across the wrist, his sword dropping uselessly from his hand.

Dazed, he staggered back, heard Deborah scream, and then was struck again. He was vaguely conscious of Deborah flinging herself forward, trying to shield him; of one of his attackers seizing her and dragging her away, still screaming. There was blood trickling down his face, a red mist before his eyes. He felt himself falling . . .

In his lodgings in the Cockpit at Whitehall, Sir Francis Wiley, Gentleman of the Bedchamber to His Majesty, was entertaining a few friends to supper, and afterwards to cards.

He was a good host and saw to it that his guests were amply provided with all they could wish for in the way of liquid refreshment. Deborah and Philip would have recognised him at once as the red-headed young gentleman who had been present that morning in Long Street, as had several of the others.

It was upon the morning's incident that the conversation had turned.

"I declare," Sir Francis said a trifle thickly, "the confounded fellow expected Howard to receive him with open arms, pack up his gear and depart, just like that." He attempted to click his fingers without success, gave up in disgust, and reached instead for his wine-glass. "Who's for some more wine? – Charles, you're not drinking tonight! What's amiss?"

Before Charles could answer, a florid-faced gentleman interposed swiftly, "My dear Francis, Charles hasn't yet recovered from this morning's affair."

"Why hasn't he?" someone demanded.

"Because of the girl, you knucklehead. Don't you remember? Met her in St. James's Park. Rescued her from the crowd. Most touching."

Charles's face was expressionless, but James, sitting nearby, saw the sudden spark of anger in his eyes and said quickly, "Leave it, Harry. Francis, where's that wine you promised us?"

Sir Francis, apologising hastily, shouted to his servant, Milsom, to bring more bottles, and when he had done so told his guests to help themselves.

With much laughter and bickering, they did so. James, looking round for Charles, discovered him standing at one of the windows, his back to the room. He joined him.

"You are not yourself tonight, Charles."

The other did not reply at once. James looked at his brooding expression and sought for something to say. Before he had succeeded, however, Charles said abruptly, "I am thinking of leaving. Will you come with me?"

A few minutes later, followed by the expostulations of their host, they left. Milsom had been sent to fetch his lordship's coach, and they were soon bowling away from Whitehall.

"Are you worried about what happened this morning?" asked James, after they had gone some way in silence.

Charles stirred. "Yes, I am. I cannot get it out of my head that Philip Wyngarde spoke the truth. Oh, I know the whole thing sounded preposterous at the time, but the more I think about it, the more convinced I am that he may be the rightful heir after all."

"Perhaps," James said doubtfully. "On the other hand, he and his sister may well be the late Baron's bastards, as

Howard suggested. Why, everyone knows his uncle's two children were reported to have been killed."

"Not *killed*, James. It was said they died of a fever. And the report of their deaths may have been put about to safeguard them, as Wyngarde asserted."

"You were as unconvinced as the rest of us this morning."

"I know, but after turning the matter over in my mind, I've come to the conclusion that I was wrong. I want to see them and discuss the matter with them. Do you wish to come with me, or shall I take you home first?"

James blinked. "*Now*? But do you know where they are lodging?"

"At the Gilded Peacock in Holborn. It's not too late to call there. What do you say? Are you coming?"

James regarded him with an expression of exasperated affection. "Of course. You know I am!"

Charles thrust his head out and shouted directions to his coachman. The heavy vehicle was soon on its way to Holborn.

"How is Helen?" James asked, settling himself more comfortably.

In the gloom it was difficult to see his friend's expression clearly, but he detected a certain note of amusement in Charles's tone as he replied that she was well enough, as far as he knew.

"What do you mean by that?" James demanded.

"Oh – nothing. She is out this evening. She had an invitation to supper at the Mulgroves'."

"With Aveling as escort? I thought you were planning to put a stop to the association?"

"Did you?" Charles countered evasively. "As it happens, young Gilroy called to take her this evening. It seems Aveling was – ah – unavoidably detained."

At this moment the coach came to a sudden halt.

"What the devil!" exclaimed Charles, and thrust his head out. "What's wrong, Danby?"

"My lord . . . listen! 'Tis a woman screaming! Like as not she's been set upon by padders."

Charles was already out of the coach. The street was dark, the narrow lane from which the sound had come even darker. With James on his heels, and Danby bringing up the rear with his whip, he checked momentarily, focussing his eyes on the grim scene.

Upon the ground lay an inert figure, a man standing over him, cudgel raised; nearby stood another man, holding a struggling girl in his arms. Even as Charles started forward, he saw her break free and throw herself down over the fallen figure, shielding him from the blow that was aimed at him, only to be struck down by it herself.

"Misbegotten rogues!" Charles sprang to the attack, sword in hand; with James, similarly armed, at his heels. They proceeded to lay about them. The two ruffians, taken by surprise, made a feeble attempt to defend themselves, but were soon overpowered. One, slashed across the wrist, gave a howl of pain, then dropped his cudgel and turned, fleeing into the darkness. His fellow, finding himself deserted, wasted no time in following suit.

"So much for *them*!" Charles sheathed his sword and turned his attention to the victims of the attack. Dropping down on one knee, he raised the unconscious girl up against him. "I don't think she's badly hurt, but that's no thanks to those . . ." His voice died away.

James, who with Danby beside him was bending over the other figure, glanced up. "What is it, Charles?"

At that moment footsteps approached the end of the lane and came to a halt.

"What's amiss here?" growled a voice. The footsteps shuffled towards them, a glow of light bobbing along with them. It was the watch, lantern on pole, dog at his heels.

"'Slight!" he exclaimed. "Who did this, then?"

"A couple of rogues who'd be better swinging at the end of a rope," Charles replied crisply. "Bring that lantern nearer! James, do you see who it is?"

"'Sblood! – Mr. Wyngarde and his sister!"

In the lantern light, Charles's expression was grim. He looked up at his friend. "Someone is at the back of this!"

"You don't mean . . ."

Charles gave a quick glance at the watchman. "It remains to be seen. . . . Help me lift them into the coach, James. I'm taking them home with me."

With Danby's assistance, they managed to carry them to the coach and lift them inside. Within a minute or two, the coach was moving slowly away, leaving the watchman standing there, staring after it. Then, with a shake of his head, he shuffled away down the street, his lantern bobbing on his shoulder, the dog padding at his heels.

CHAPTER SIX

SLOWLY, Deborah returned to consciousness.

She was aware, first, of a throbbing, nagging pain in her head. She moaned, and found that she was resting against something warm and smooth; and also that she was being jolted along in some kind of vehicle. For a moment she thought dazedly she must be in the stagecoach . . . though surely they had reached London by this time?

Forcing her eyes open, she tried to focus them, but could see little save a vague shape in the darkness, a shape that came close and hung over her, while a man's voice murmured, "I think she's recovered consciousness."

Then she remembered. The footsteps coming after them, the rush of blows that had beaten Philip to the ground; the man who had held her. . . . She had torn herself free to go to Philip's aid, and then something had hit her with agonising force on the head, and the world had rushed away from her into whirling darkness.

Those men! Philip. . . .

There were arms about her, holding her. She began to struggle, trying to free herself, turning her head from side to side, her breath coming in little gasps.

"No . . . no! Please!"

"Calm yourself, Mistress Deborah." It was that same voice. "You are quite safe now."

"Safe?" She peered up at him, but could see little of his face. "How did you know my name?" The words were scarcely audible.

"We have met before," he assured her.

There was a movement from the other side of the coach. Deborah turned her head. "Philip?"

"He is here," said another voice.

She tried to raise herself, to sit upright, but the arms round her restrained her, and the soft voice told her to remain still, he was taking them home, all would be well. She was not to worry. He would take care of everything.

"Thank you," she breathed, scarcely knowing what she was saying, but blessedly aware, now that her panic had subsided, of being protected and cared for, of those comforting arms holding her close, of the warmth and strength of him.

In a little while the coach came to a halt. She opened her heavy eyes again, and lifted her head from his shoulder.

There was a sudden draught of cool air as the coach door was opened. Strong arms lifted her out, and light streamed from an open door, down a broad flight of steps. She was carried into that river of light; it hurt her eyes, so she closed them and let her cheek fall against that comforting shoulder once more. There were voices, sharp with alarm; hurrying footsteps of servants rushing past and down the steps.

"Careful! Careful with his head! Steady now . . . that's right . . . Danby, go at once for Dr. Graham. Tell him it's urgent. Yes, yes, carry him upstairs. Matthew . . . where's Matthew? Oh, there you are. Take charge of him, will you? And find Rose. Tell her to bring warm water and towels and some ointment – Thank you, James. Yes, in here."

She was being carried across a hall and into a room warm with comfort, with the scent of roses. She was set gently down upon a day-bed on which was a soft mattress covered with cushions. Again she closed her eyes, for it was too much of an effort to keep them open. For a while time had no meaning for her; then she was aware of someone smoothing her hair away from her forehead, and dabbing something wet and warm upon it. Her face puckered. She blinked and looked up.

"I'm sorry, mistress. I will try not to hurt you."

A fresh-faced young woman in neat attire. A servant; but a superior servant, for her hands were soft and well-kept, her voice pleasantly modulated

"Who are you?" queried Deborah.

"My name is Rose. I am her ladyship's tiring-maid."

She was drying Deborah's forehead and cheek with a soft damask towel, gently, carefully.

Deborah frowned. "Her ladyship?"

Rose had picked up a small jar, and was now applying ointment to the ugly bruise on Deborah's forehead.

"Lady Revett," she said, and then, "There. I think that'll do." She surveyed the bruise for a moment, and clucked over it. "The villains! No one's safe in the streets at night. Do you lie still. I think his lordship is bringing you something to revive you."

"His lordship is," said another voice, and he was there beside her, gazing down at her with that deep, dark expression she found so hard to meet.

Rose moved aside, and Charles bent over Deborah, slipping an arm beneath her shoulders. He held out a glass. "Drink this. 'Tis only wine. The cook is going to make you a hot posset. You shall have it in a little while."

Obediently she took the glass and sipped the wine.

"You are very kind," she murmured, giving the glass back to him.

He smiled slightly. "Are you comfortable? Would you like a wrap? Rose . . ."

"Yes, my lord. I'll fetch one."

As she went out, there came the sound of brisk knocking upon the outer door, which was opened at once. Voices . . . the door closing. Hurried steps across the hall. A tap on the door.

"Dr. Graham, my lord."

The doctor entered on the footman's heels; a man in his thirties, of medium height, quietly dressed, with a grave, enquiring expression on his thin face.

Charles greeted him. "It was good of you to come so soon, Doctor."

"Danby assured me it was urgent. Is this my patient?"

He came to stand beside the day-bed, and raised his brows at Deborah, who struggled into a sitting position, and then uttered an involuntary whimper of pain and put a hand to her head. He peered at the bruise, while Charles apprised him briefly of what had occurred.

"Dear me! How fortunate you happened to arrive on the scene at such a timely moment – I'm sorry. Did that hurt?" This to Deborah, who had winced away from his probing fingers. "Nothing serious, though it's a bad bruise. I'll send the boy round with a draught to help you sleep." He straightened. "And now I'll go upstairs and take a look at your brother. You remain here for the moment."

"Can I not come with you?" Her eyes beseeched him.

"You shall come up in a little while," he assured her, smiling, and with that she had to be content.

As he and Charles went towards the door, Rose entered, carrying a warm wrap.

"Ah, good!" said Charles. "Look after her, Rose. I must go upstairs with Dr. Graham." With a reassuring smile at Deborah he left the room, ushering the doctor out before him.

Feeling a little lost, Deborah allowed the maid to fuss over her, and lay quietly, eyes half-closed, trying to ignore the stabbing pain in her head. The wrap, of palest pink, was soft and silky warm with a trace of some elusive perfume about it, very pleasing to her nostrils.

"Who," she enquired carefully "is Lady Revett?"

Rose, having seated herself on a low stool with a tapestry-covered cushion, informed her that her ladyship was Lord Mulgarth's sister, a widow, to whom he was at present acting in the capacity of guardian.

"Oh," murmured Deborah; and strangely, she found comfort in this information.

For a while she remained silent, then, as something occurred to her, she asked whether there had been another gentleman in the coach.

"Oh yes, mistress. That would be Sir James Leveson. His lordship asked him to go and fetch your things from the Gilded Peacock – yours and your brother's, that is. He went as soon as Danby came back with the doctor."

"Our things! – But Mrs. Goffin will never allow him to take them . . . not unless he pays the reckoning!"

"Don't you fret about that!" said Rose soothingly. "His lordship will have thought of it. He'll have told Sir James to pay it, and settle with him later."

"He is very kind."

The maid gave her a somewhat odd look. Then, with a humorous twist of the lips, she agreed that he was, *very*.

It was some time before Deborah was summoned upstairs and with Rose's assistance, made her way up to the bedchamber to which Philip had been carried.

She found him lying in the great fourposter, head swathed in bandages, face colourless, eyes closed. He had not regained consciousness. To Deborah, seating herself on the stool by his bedside, it seemed that his life hung in the balance, so still was he, so shallow his breathing. His hand, lying on the silken coverlet, was ice-cold to the touch.

Dr. Graham, in answer to her look of entreaty, assured her that he had seen men in far worse straits than her brother, all of whom had managed to survive. His injuries, though serious, could have been far worse. He was suffering from concussion, and was fortunate, said the doctor, not to have sustained a cracked skull. With God's help he would mend.

He then joined Lord Mulgarth at the foot of the bed, conversing with him in low tones. Deborah caught the word "fever", and bit her lip hard. Rose, standing beside her, gave her a quick, reassuring smile.

All at once, the doctor checked his words, glancing towards the closed door. Charles jerked his head in the same direction, listened, and then strode towards it. Deborah heard swift footsteps approaching, and then, without warning, the door crashed back on its hinges. Framed in the doorway stood a young woman, swaying slightly.

Deborah blinked, and stared, her gaze taking in the dark hair dressed in elaborate curls that fell upon bare shoulders and bosom, the blue eyes that glittered in the painted face, the flash of jewels, the shimmering gown of silver satin, sewn with pearls, the richly-embroidered under-petticoat above high heels and slender ankles. To Deborah's confused mind she appeared to be some glorious being from another world. It took her a moment to realise who she was – the young woman whose life Philip had saved in Hyde Park. So this, then, was Helen – Lady Revett, sister to his lordship!

"Charles! What has happened? They told me some rigmarole downstairs of an – an accident."

Her voice, imperious in tone, was slurred. As she moved forward, she swayed, and Deborah saw Lord Mulgarth grip her arm.

"Yes, there *has* been an accident, Helen. There is nothing you can do, however, so I suggest you allow Rose to prepare you for bed."

The words were spoken quietly, albeit in a tone that brooked no argument. Her ladyship evidently thought otherwise. Pulling herself free and breathing rapidly, she said in the same loud, imperious tones, "Leave me! I do not wish to retire . . . 'tis early yet! Let me . . ."

She made as though to sweep past him, but he caught her by the shoulders, spun her round to face him and said between his teeth, "Helen, you will go at once! – *Rose!*"

The maid was already beside them. "Come, my lady," she said soothingly. "You are tired."

"I am not tired! Damn you! Damn you, Charles! *Let me go!*"

Deborah had half risen from her stool when a sound from the bed brought her gaze back to Philip, and she promptly forgot all else. His head moved fractionally, his pale lips uttered a low moan. Immediately the doctor came forward and bent over him.

"He's coming round."

Philip's lids fluttered, his eyes opened. "Deborah?"

"I'm here, Philip." She pressed his limp hand, and he turned his head on the pillow, looking up at her.

His lips moved. Bending towards him, she was just able to make out the words, "Thank God!" His eyes closed.

Deborah glanced up at Dr. Graham in mute appeal. He

shook his head, and put a hand on her shoulder in encouragement. "Leave him until tomorrow. Do not expect more of him now. You must give him time."

She nodded blindly and groped for her kerchief, then was conscious of a sudden rustling of silken skirts, of a little gasp. Looking up, she found Lady Revett beside her, staring in utter disbelief at Philip.

"Charles!" Helen turned swiftly to her brother, her voice all at once clear and low, as though shock had sobered her. "This is Mr. Ryall . . . the man who saved me when my horse bolted. You remember? I told you . . ."

Dr. Graham broke in swiftly. "With all deference, I think it would be advisable for you to leave now, my lady, and allow the patient to rest."

"Of course. I'm sorry."

She permitted Charles to lead her away, and they conversed together in low tones for a moment in the doorway. Then, with a quick glance in Deborah's direction, she left the room with Rose in attendance.

Charles returned to the bedside and smiled down at Deborah. "Come, you must rest too."

"But Philip—"

"He will not be left alone, I promise you. Someone will stay with him all the time."

Thus reassured, Deborah allowed him to lead her from the bedchamber and down the stairs, back to the room into which he had carried her on bringing her into the house. A little later the doctor bowed himself out, promising to call in the morning, and she was left alone with his lordship.

"You are tired," he said gently. "Rose will come for you soon, to assist you to bed."

She tried to smile, but failed. "Thank you."

He saw that she was close to tears. "My poor little one. . . ."

His arms went round her; he drew her against him. She felt once again the warmth of his comfort and protection, a cloak against the remembered horror of that vicious attack in the dark lane. He rested his cheek lightly against her forehead for a moment before, very gently, touching it with his lips. She raised her eyes to his, and he read doubt and uncertainty in them.

Sensing her withdrawal, he let her go, and she moved away from him, seating herself on the edge of the day-bed, hands clasped tightly in her lap.

"This morning . . . you did not believe Philip, did you? Even though you suggested that he might have documents to prove his claim, you weren't *really* convinced. You thought the same as everybody else – that we were impostors, trying to cozen Howard." Her tone was bitter, her expression accusing.

"Deborah, let me explain." He seated himself on the stool. "It is true, I *did* doubt your brother's story. At the time it sounded so fantastic! Knowing Howard, and having met your father . . ."

"You *met* him? Where was this?"

"In Brussels. Like Howard, I chose to leave home to live in voluntary exile, having quarrelled with my father over the match he had made for Helen. I came to know your father well. He lived for the day when he could return home. He was always talking about Wyngarde Court. It meant a lot to him. He had heard how his cousin had sacked the place, but his intention was to restore it to its former glory. The King had given him his word that action would be taken against Francis Wyngarde to make him bear the full costs of such a restoration – he was, of course, well able to do so. You are doubtless aware that he owned a prosperous estate of his own in Buckinghamshire, and had also been well rewarded for his services to Parliament by the grant of sequestered estates formerly belonging to Royalists."

"I had heard something of that." She had been listening intently, a frown between her brows. "So it seems Howard is a wealthy man?"

"He has stated that he intends to return the sequestered estates to their former owners, or to their descendants, wherever possible. Even so . . . yes, I suppose he can be accounted wealthy. His father was able to buy up a good deal of property over the years. Impoverished Royalists were forced to sell land in order to meet their fines." He paused, and then continued in lighter tones, "As I said, the King had promised to recompense your father. His Majesty was always free with his promises, and still is. He promises more than he can justifiably fulfil. Nevertheless, I believe he truly appreciated your father's worth and in his case, really meant what he said. It so happened that he did not have to meet his pledge."

"No." Deborah's eyes clouded.

He gave her a reflective look. "Deborah, you and your brother knew that Lord Wyngarde was safe in exile, yet you never once got in touch with him. You let him believe you were dead. All those years, and not one letter. Is it any wonder your brother's story was received with such doubt and disbelief?"

"John Ryall, the cousin who brought us up, thought it would be better if we remained silent. He feared not only for our safety, but for our father's if it became known that we were still alive. Colonel Wyngarde was a vindictive man. He would have stopped at nothing."

"I have heard he had a violent disposition, though I never met him."

"But you came to know Howard in exile, and became his friend?"

"That is so, though our friendship was never a close one."

"Close enough for you to visit him in his – his house in London."

Charles acknowledged the thrust with a slight inclination of the head.

She rushed on, "He gained your trust, and I suppose the King's. Unless we can find those documents, he will remain Lord Wyngarde...." Her voice broke; she bowed her head, fighting for composure. "And you, and all the others will continue to – to trust him, and to treat us as impostors...."

"No, Deborah!" He put a firm hand over hers. "Ever since this morning I have been unable to get you out of my mind, wondering if, after all, we were mistaken in our rejection of your brother's claim. Indeed, I felt so strongly about it that I was actually on my way to call upon you both this evening, to talk over the matter with you."

He told her how he and James had left their friend's lodging and set out for Holborn; and how Danby, hearing her screams, had stopped the coach. "We made short work of those villains." His tone was grim. "They'll not be so eager to attack defenceless people in future."

"Philip did have his sword, but had no chance to use it."

"Danby found it lying on the ground. We brought it back with us."

"I suppose they intended to rob us." She gave a little wry smile. "What would they have said, I wonder, if they had known we had not a penny between us?" She told him about the pickpocket. He listened closely, and then asked her to repeat the description of the man.

"I will see what can be done about finding him," he remarked. "Is it possible for you to describe the others to me? You would not have seen them very clearly."

"I – I don't know," she said uncertainly. "There was a man . . . he followed us into the Mitre, when we went to find Mr. Osborne."

"Mr. Osborne?" His brows lifted.

She explained briefly.

"Edward Osborne," he murmured slowly, and then shook his head. "No, I cannot place him, though I have the feeling I've heard the name before. You may rest assured, however, that I shall do my best to bring those two knaves to justice!"

She gave a little shudder. His hand tightened over hers. "You have nothing to fear now, Deborah. You will be safe under my roof."

"We . . . we cannot impose upon you."

"Impose?" His eyes held hers. "Don't you know . . ."

He broke off as someone tapped on the door. In answer to his impatient summons, Rose entered. Her ladyship was in bed; she would now be pleased to assist Mistress Deborah.

"Very well, Rose." Charles's tone was curt. Rose, with swift perception, smiled and retreated into the hall, where she could be heard chaffing the footman who waited there against Sir James's return.

Charles got to his feet, drawing Deborah up with him. "You and your brother will remain here, as my guests, for as long as you both wish . . . and certainly until he is fully recovered. As for imposing upon me, you are doing no such thing! When I think what might have happened to you tonight. . . ."

He could not trust himself to continue. Instead his arm went round her and, bending his head, his lips touched hers; and then, with commendable restraint, he let her go.

CHAPTER SEVEN

HELEN, Lady Revett, lay awake, staring blindly into the soft darkness within the bed-curtains, eyes red and swollen with weeping, in her heart a knot of misery.

'Finished,' she thought. 'Finished . . . just like that! And he . . . he scarcely looked at me all the evening. He could not face me. He knew what everyone was saying behind our backs.'

She heard them again – the whispers, the sniggers, the sly gibes – none of them addressed directly to her, but intended for her ears, nevertheless. She beat at the coverlet with clenched fists, as she might have struck against their faces; the faces which, all evening, had watched her and George Aveling . . . and his wife.

It seemed she had lain awake for hours, going over it again and again. Her thoughts were trapped in that circle of remembering, from the moment *they* had arrived, and she had heard her hostess, Lady Mulgrove, exclaim in blank surprise, "Elizabeth! I didn't know you were back in London!" And she had turned, and across the room had met George's eyes, wary and guarded; and had been aware in that same moment of a certain stillness, as though everybody was waiting to see what she would do.

Had they been disappointed when she had turned back to Jack Gilroy with some quick remark, and the moment had passed? Pride had come to her aid then, pride and a determination not to give them the satisfaction of knowing that her whole being felt rigid with shock, as though she had become encased in ice.

Pride had carried her through the rest of the evening. She had smiled and laughed, had even managed to converse with a certain brittle gaiety; while all the time she had been aware of *her*, the pretty, charming little creature by George's side. Elizabeth Aveling, who had been conveniently recuperating after the birth of her first child, a girl, in the depths of the country. Now, it seemed, she had decided to return to London, leaving her baby daughter in the care of a reliable wet-nurse; and, accompanied by her mother, had travelled back to George's side.

Staring into the darkness, Helen thought bitterly of those she had called her friends, the people she had come to know through George. She saw them now for what they were . . . idle pleasure-seekers amusing themselves at the expense of others, filling empty hours with empty amusement. And she, flattered by George's overwhelming attentions, and by their admiring and fulsome compliments, had allowed herself to drift with them along the same paths.

She recalled that George had barely spoken to her all the evening. He had not even presented her to his wife, whom she had known slightly when they had both been children, but had left it to Lady Mulgrove to do so. They had smiled and kissed each other on the cheek, while the whole room had looked on.

Elizabeth had said something, to which she had replied. She could not recall their words, but she could still see Elizabeth's face, with its dimpled cheeks and guileless eyes that had . . . oh, now she was certain of it! . . . held a faintly derisive, faintly pitying expression.

Turning over, she buried her face in the soft down pillow Elizabeth had known!

By tomorrow it would be the talk of London; would, without doubt, reach Charles's ears. She could expect no sympathy from him. Had he not told her she was a fool to fall so completely beneath George Aveling's spell? He was nothing but a blackguard, a worthless rake. Charles had done his best to make her promise never to see him again. He had even threatened to send her to their grandfather if she persisted in allowing him to pay court to her. She had merely tossed her head at him. Was *he* any better than George? she had demanded hotly. Yet, in her heart of hearts, she had known that Charles was right. Even as she lay there, sick with misery, some inner voice told her that everything had happened for the best, that she was well rid of George.

She thought of his blandishments, his kisses and caresses. She had been aware from the beginning that with him she was playing with fire. The knowledge had added spice to the relationship. She had known of his reputation, of course, and yet there was something about him that had blinded her to the truth . . . or had she deliberately shut her mind to it, telling herself that *this* time he was sincere, *this* time he really meant it when he said she was the only woman in the world for him, that his marriage had been a terrible mistake. . . ?

Helen's lip curled in the darkness. How many other women had he said that to? Disillusioned, bitter, she told herself that never again would she allow herself to be so easily deceived, so ready to give her heart. And she might thank Providence, said that inner voice, that that was *all* she had given.

She moved her head restlessly on the pillow. How it ached! She had drunk far too much wine. It had helped to sustain her through that interminable evening. Jack Gilroy had brought her home. She had a vague remembrance of him pressing kisses on her unwilling lips. Poor Jack! He made his adoration plain, but she knew she would never feel any more than a certain fondness for him, any more than she would for James, who was equally devoted to her.

She recalled the scene in the bedchamber. She had behaved badly. Charles had been furious with her. She could remember his face, his fingers digging into her arm as he had tried to restrain her. And the man lying in the bed. The very last person she had expected to see. Philip Ryall. . . . But Rose had said that his name was Wyngarde, that he and his sister had been set upon by thieves, and had been rescued by Charles and James.

Why had Charles brought them back here? And why had they taken the name "Wyngarde"?

In the book-room, Charles and James were deep in discussion, James having returned from Holborn some time before.

Brows drawn together, he said: "What did you mean when you said someone was behind the attack?"

"I should have thought that was obvious! Supposing you were Howard, enjoying a comfortable position with a host of influential friends, and on the best of terms with the King: and then without warning some outsider, of whose existence you had been totally unaware, suddenly appeared and claimed that he should be in your place. Would you not do all in your power to stop him? And, knowing that he intended to leave London as soon as possible in order to fetch the documents which would substantiate his claim, wouldn't you act at once?"

His friend's expression was one of profound astonishment. "You cannot be serious, Charles!"

"I am not saying *you* would do it, but Howard is perfectly capable of behaving in such a manner. This morning I happened to be standing at the window of his room when Philip and Deborah Wyngarde went out into the street. They were followed."

"What!"

"If you remember, Howard had a word with Terris in the hall. Shortly afterwards I saw a man leave the house and hurry after the Wyngardes. It seems clear to me he was acting under orders to follow them back to their lodgings, and probably to keep watch on their movements, and report back."

"What about the pickpocket? Surely *he* wasn't in league with the others?"

"He could have been. In any event I intend to have him found, together with those two villains, and brought to me for questioning."

"How will you find them?"

"I shall leave it to Matthew." Matthew was Charles's personal servant, a man of complete reliability, who had been in his service for a number of years, and had insisted upon accompanying him to Flanders, where he had proved an invaluable asset.

"Where will he start?"

"The Mitre in Fleet Street would be as good a place as any. It plays quite a part in this affair. According to Mistress Deborah, it was where Mr. Osborne first took her brother, and where she and Mr. Wyngarde went this evening in search of him to see if he would advance them some money. While they were there, she saw a man who might have been one of their attackers. He was joined by a woman, whom Mistress Deborah has described to me. I think Matthew might obtain some useful information from *her*."

"I wonder if she would know the pickpocket, too?"

"It's probable. Birds of a feather . . ." Charles rubbed his chin reflectively. "I have a strong feeling that Mr. Osborne might be mixed up in this business."

"Oh come, Charles!" James's eyes twinkled. "You told me a short while ago that Mistress Deborah spoke of him as someone who had a fondness for her! Besides, what possible connection could he have with Howard?"

"I don't know yet; but if Howard *is* at the bottom of this business, he will be answerable to me!"

When Deborah awoke next morning she could not, for the moment, remember where she was.

She blinked up at the ornamented tester above her head, and then at the hangings of the bed, blue velvet lined with white silk, a puzzled frown on her brow. This was not the bed she had slept in at the Gilded Peacock, nor was it her own bed at Hallowden.

Raising her head from the soft pillow she became at once aware of a dull ache and put up her hand, wincing as her fingers touched her forehead.

And then she remembered.

She sat up with a swift glance at the embroidered quilt, stretched out a hand and, pulling aside the bed-curtain, peeped out into the room.

It was large. To her muddled mind, still hazy with the

after-effects of the sleeping draught Dr. Graham had prescribed for her, it seemed to stretch away into infinite distance, filled with heavy carved oak furniture, a fringed carpet on the floor beside the bed, a couple of padded stools, curtains matching the bed-hangings pulled across the windows.

Pushing aside the covers, Deborah swung her feet over the edge of the bed, sitting there for a moment until her head had cleared a little; then she looked down at herself. She was clad in a garment she had never seen before, a smock of gossamer-fine lawn with layers of lace inset into bodice and sleeves, and silk ribbons adorning it. Standing up, she moved across to the windows to draw back the curtains. As she did so she caught sight of a dim figure out of the corner of her eye, moving in like fashion.

She stopped dead, heart pounding, and then gave a small shaky laugh. It was her own reflection in a mirror hanging on the wall.

She pulled the curtains open, letting in a flood of brilliant sunshine. There was a garden below, so the bedchamber must be at the back of the house. A beautiful garden with an arbour, and a little pool in which stood a fat, naked Cupid holding aloft a fluted vessel from which water continually flowed.

Turning away from the window, she crossed to the mirror. It must be one of the new French ones, for she had never seen its like before. The frame was gilded and ornamented with delicately-carved flowers and leaves – altogether, an exquisite piece of work.

The face that looked back at her was pale and heavy-eyed, her forehead swollen and disfigured by the bruise. Perhaps she would be able to hide it beneath her hair, she thought.

She froze suddenly. Someone was coming!

Scampering back to the bed, she dived into it and pulled the covers up to her chin just as the door opened. In came Rose, carrying a ewer of water which she set down on the toilet table. Turning, she saw that Deborah was awake, and bobbed a smiling curtsey.

"Good morrow, mistress. I hope I didn't disturb you, but the doctor has arrived and wishes to see you when he has attended to Mr. Wyngarde."

"Oh!" Deborah was immediately alert. "How is my brother this morning?"

Rose, swishing back the rest of the bed-curtains, replied that according to Blake, the servant who was tending him, his condition remained the same.

She then said, "Did you sleep well, mistress? I see you have already been out of bed." She gave a significant nod towards the windows and then, as Deborah sat up, arranged the pillows comfortably behind her before pouring water from the ewer into the silver bowl which, together with a damask towel, she brought to the bedside.

Deborah bathed her face and hands. "What time is it?" she asked and was shocked to learn that it was already approaching the hour of ten.

Rose, deftly brushing and tidying her hair, told her not to worry. Lady Revett was still asleep, and would probably not stir until noon, for it was likely she had had a bad night. Having made this pronouncement, Rose compressed her lips tightly together, as though she could have added something more but felt constrained not to do so.

A scratch on the door heralded the arrival of Dr. Graham, who came briskly into the room, bidding Deborah a smiling "Good morrow!" Having enquired whether she had slept well, he bent and examined the bruise.

"Hm. Yes, it's coming out. Have you a headache? – I thought so. Do your eyes hurt? – We'll have those curtains closed, if you please." This to Rose, who flew to obey him. "I'll make you up something to ease your head, and send it round. Rest as much as you can today. I will call in again tomorrow."

"Dr. Graham, how is my brother?"

"At the moment, barely conscious. But—" as she drew in her breath sharply "—he's strong. He'll pull through."

"You said he might succumb to fever." Deborah's voice faltered and died away.

"'Tis a natural after-effect. Nothing to worry about." His tone was reassuring.

She plucked at the sheet. "Will you have to bleed him?"

"Only if it will help to relieve the fever. I shall, of course, put him on a light diet. No strong liquor, no red meat. He should be over the worst in a few days." He smiled at her again, bade her "Good day!" and left.

"I suggest, mistress, that you remain in bed for the moment." Rose was at the bedside. "Phoebe will bring you up a morning draught, and later a light dinner."

Rose, it seemed, had her own ideas concerning the treatment of semi-invalids, and Deborah, who had been about to suggest tentatively that she would like to get up and visit her brother's room, felt unequal to the task of arguing the point with her. Instead she relaxed against the pillows, and later sipped her ale and ate a little thinly-sliced bread and butter.

Rose took away the tray, leaving her to sleep, but instead of doing so Deborah found her thoughts returning to the man who, ever since her first meeting with him, had occupied them practically to the exclusion of everything else ... Lord Mulgarth. With a little sigh, she half-closed her eyes, recalling the strength and comfort of his arms, the way he had looked at her; above all, his kiss that, for all its gentleness, had held more than a hint of restrained passion.

She had never been kissed like that before – stirring her blood, setting her pulses throbbing wildly. A disturbing, frightening sensation. How could she, inexperienced as she was, ever hope to analyse it?

She recalled his assurance that she and Philip were to remain under his roof for as long as they wished, and wondered how long that would be. Once Philip had recovered, he would be in haste to return to Hallowden for the papers. Even without that end in view, she doubted very much whether he would consent to stay in the house a moment longer than was absolutely necessary. He had made his opinion of Lord Mulgarth perfectly plain to her.

Her thoughts strayed to Lady Revett. How startled Philip

would be to learn that she was Lord Mulgarth's sister! Though he had not spoken of her since he saw her at the playhouse, having casually mentioned the encounter afterwards, she suspected that his thoughts had often strayed in that direction. Well, she was certainly a lovely creature, but remembering the events of the previous night, Deborah felt that her behaviour then had left much to be desired.

Phoebe, plump and pretty, a little younger than Rose, brought in her dinner – slices of chicken in a creamy sauce, served with a green sallet, and a spiced custard to follow.

Having eaten, Deborah drifted off into a half-sleep, from which she was roused by a soft scratching on the door. Lady Revett entered, and on seeing that Deborah was awake, advanced into the room, smiling.

"I hoped I should find you awake. I thought it was time we became acquainted. You are Deborah Wyngarde, are you not? I am Helen Revett."

"Yes, I know. My brother has . . . has spoken of you."

Deborah regarded her shyly. Helen's thick hair was hanging loosely down her back, a blue ribbon round her head. Her face was very pale and, as she approached the bed, Deborah saw that there were dark shadows round her eyes, giving them a bruised look. The corners of her full mouth drooped. She was clad in a floating garment of fine white lawn, diaphanous and very becoming to her tall, graceful figure. On her feet she wore silk slippers.

She surveyed Deborah with frank interest. "You bear a certain likeness to your brother, I think. May I sit on the bed?"

"Please do."

Helen seated herself with a sigh, pressing her hands for a moment over her eyes.

"Are you not well?" Deborah enquired solicitously.

Helen shrugged. "It will pass. 'Tis as well the curtains are drawn. I feel positively haggard and must certainly appear so."

"Oh, no! Indeed you do not."

Helen gave her a rueful smile. "You are flattering me, I'm sure. And now, pray enlighten me as to what happened last night; unless, that is, you find it too painful to do so. Rose did tell me something about it, but I fear I remember very little of what she said."

Deborah told her and Helen, drawing her feet up beneath her, listened with keen interest.

"The villains!" she exclaimed. "Thank heaven, Charles and James arrived in time. Otherwise . . ." She broke off, with a shudder.

"Otherwise," Deborah finished quietly, "Philip might have been killed."

They looked at each in sombre silence, then Helen leaned forward and put her hand over Deborah's for a moment. "Try not to worry."

She slipped off the bed and wandered over to the mirror, where she stood eyeing her reflection critically. Then, with a shrug, she turned away and going to the window, pulled aside a curtain and looked out.

"It is a lovely afternoon. Would you care to rest in the garden? We could sit in the arbour, or take some cushions out beneath the trees. Yes! We'll do that!"

She was all at once a different person, eyes alight, cheeks tinged with colour. Her enthusiasm was infectious, but Deborah was disconcerted to discover that she was expected to wear nothing more than slippers and an undress gown similar to that worn by Helen.

The latter was amused by her dismayed expression, assuring her that no one would see her, save perhaps a servant or two. "Charles has gone out and will not be back until later; and we won't be disturbed, for I shall give orders that I am not receiving any callers."

Deborah allowed herself to be persuaded, but expressed the wish that she would like to see Philip before going into the garden. Helen took her to his room, which was dim and quiet. Blake, sitting by the bedside, rose as they entered. Deborah looked down at her brother. He was still unconscious, his cheeks bearing a sunken appearance, his breathing shallow.

Tears pricked her eyes, and Helen put a comforting arm about her shoulders.

"Do not distress yourself. He is in good hands."

Despite her reassuring words, there was a catch in her voice. Deborah, glancing at her, saw a tremor cross her face, and wondered.

Once in the garden, however, Helen recovered her volatile spirits, and both girls settled themselves comfortably on the cushions piled in the welcome shade of the trees where, reclining side by side, they whiled away the afternoon in companionable discourse.

At Helen's request, Deborah told her about Hallowden, and how she and Philip had come to live there in the care of John Ryall, taking his name for safety's sake. She told her of the sack of their own home, and the tragic death of their mother; and how, with the restoration of the King, they had come to London to find their father. Their delight when they had believed him to be alive, their dismay when they learned the truth.

"What a shock it must have been," Helen sympathised, adding: "And I suppose it came as an equal shock for Howard, when you suddenly confronted him. That doubtless explains his discourtesy towards you. He is generally so pleasant and gracious."

"I did not realise you knew him."

"Oh, yes! He is a friend of Charles's. They met in Flanders while they were in exile. Strange to say, they both chose to leave England after quarrelling with their respective fathers – Howard because of his father's stringent political views, and Charles because *our* father insisted on marrying me to a man who was utterly debauched."

"How terrible for you!" Deborah was aghast.

Helen smiled. "Not really! My charming husband drank himself to death within a year; and as I was but fifteen at the time, we never lived together as man and wife."

"Have you ever considered marrying again?"

"Perhaps – in time."

"You must have many admirers. Is there not one special one among them?" Deborah was thinking of Philip. That he held Helen in high regard she felt sure, but if Helen's heart was already given to another, it would be better for him to know before his own heart was engaged.

Helen's mouth twisted bitterly. "No! No one at all." She put an arm over her eyes for a moment, as though the soft green light that filtered through the foliage above them had suddenly become too strong.

"I'm sorry," Deborah said awkwardly. "I did not mean to pry."

Helen took her arm away. "'Tis of no consequence. Tell me – are *you* betrothed?"

"No."

"Time enough. You are young yet."

"Turned eighteen."

"And I am nearly twenty-one – and feel at least ten years older. Heigh ho! What it is to be young and daisy-fresh!" She cast a quizzical glance at Deborah. "Tell me – how did you first come to meet Charles?"

"In St. James's Park." Deborah explained the circumstances of that meeting, and Helen listened with a faint smile.

"How like him, to go to the rescue of a damsel in distress – especially one as bewitching as yourself."

Deborah flushed at the irony in the other's tone. "Does he make it a habit?"

"He might do, if he happened to be interested enough in the damsel concerned." Helen sent her another oblique glance, noting Deborah's troubled expression. It gave her food for thought, as did Deborah's next remark.

"He is not married?"

"Neither married nor betrothed."

Keeping her gaze lowered, Deborah said: "When we saw him at the playhouse, he was with a lady. She – they – seemed to be on close terms."

"That would have been Mrs. Dennis," Helen said carelessly. "She is his mistress." She spoke freely, as she would have done to her intimates, used as she was to the frank, unrestrained speech of the fashionable world, and momentarily forgetting the effect her words might have on Deborah's susceptibilities. But when she saw the sudden painful flush that stained Deborah's cheeks, she gave a rueful laugh. "Oh, lud! I shouldn't have said that!"

"It doesn't matter. I had already guessed. One expects it of a man in – in his position."

Helen's brow darkened. "What you are saying is that men are not expected to be chaste. Yet if a woman takes a lover, 'tis a different tale. She is immediately branded as a strumpet!"

With a quick, impatient movement she sat up, rearranged her cushions, and lay down again, her back to Deborah, who stared at her in consternation, conscious that something was seriously wrong and at a loss to know what to say. In the end she said nothing, deeming it wiser to remain silent.

After a while she dozed off – only to be roused by the sound of voices. Her eyes flew open. She sat up with a startled gasp, to see Charles and another gentleman advancing across the lawn.

Hastily straightening her flimsy apparel, she sent an accusing look at Helen who, correctly interpreting it, addressed her brother in severe tones. "We were not expecting you back so early! You have taken us completely by surprise."

"I apologise," Charles returned lightly. He smiled down at Deborah. "May I present Sir James Leveson? He was with me last night when we brought you and your brother back to the house, but it was an inopportune moment for introductions."

James executed a graceful bow. "My duty, Mistress Deborah. I trust you are recovering from the attack?"

"Indeed, yes." She smiled fleetingly, acutely aware of her semi-clad state, and even more aware of it when she caught Charles's perceptive gaze upon her. Helen, she saw, was quite at ease, evidently accustomed to receiving callers while *en déshabille*.

She herself was relieved when Rose appeared to announce that it wanted but an hour to supper, and perhaps the ladies would wish to retire in order to dress. They sauntered back to the house, James and Helen a little in advance of the others, exchanging easy banter. Charles's gaze followed them, a slight frown between his brows.

He glanced at Deborah. "Has Helen mentioned anything to you about last night?"

"She asked me what had happened. She didn't remember . . ."

"That does not surprise me!"

"Don't be angry with her," Deborah said quickly. "I believe she is desperately unhappy." Her glance went to the laughing girl, now entering the house on James's arm. "—For all her apparent gaiety," she added.

"I know."

Deborah looked up at him. "You do?"

Charles nodded, immeasurably conscious of her loveliness, of her tender young body beneath the filmy garments; conscious of desire stirring within him. They had halted, and he took her hand, his eyes searching her face. She was unawakened; yet he sensed the sudden awareness in her, marked by the swift rise and fall of her breasts, the dilation of her pupils as her eyes met his.

His fingers tightened round hers. Raising her hand to his lips, he kissed it. Her glance wavered, and fell. With a sighing breath, she turned and sped into the house.

As he stood there, gazing after her, James joined him.

"She's a sweet child," he observed, "though a trifle too inexperienced for your tastes."

He was startled by the sudden flash of anger in Charles's eyes. "Why? Am I past redemption?"

"No, of course not. Don't jump down my throat! I merely meant that compared with other ladies of your acquaintance, she is singularly young and artless, and would soon bore you. What attracts you at the moment is her innocence. She presents a fresh challenge. Once you have won her, she will cease to interest you."

Charles's hand shot out and fastened round James's wrist in a grip that made him wince.

"One more word and I'll break your neck! Very well – I admit I was attracted to her originally because of those qualities you mention. I admit I want her – but not in the way you infer." He released James's wrist, and as the latter rubbed it ruefully, went on: "I intend to make her my wife."

"What! 'Sblood, Charles – you can't be serious! What will your grandfather say?"

"That I've completely lost my senses, I expect. Oh, I know he won't approve. He takes it for granted that I'll make a brilliant marriage with a suitable heiress, thus carrying on the family tradition. Both he and my father did the same – but why should I follow suit? I've no need of money. Neither has Helen."

"Which is something to be thankful for." James paused, and then said carefully: "There is the question of birth, of course."

Charles flashed him a look. "I thought you might mention that."

"It's no good closing your eyes to the fact that Howard could be right. Deborah and Philip may well be his uncle's bastards; and all this talk of documents could be merely to save face."

"Have you forgotten the attack?"

"You've no proof . . ."

"Not yet – but I will have before long."

"There's another point. If their claim *is* false, the whole town will hear of it. Howard will see to that. Deborah and her brother will be a laughing-stock, and *you*, my dear Charles, will share in their disgrace if you marry the girl. Assuming, of course, that she accepts you. If she loves you, she'll probably refuse, for the sake of your good name."

"James, I'll not listen to any more of your maunderings. Deborah is no impostor, neither is her brother. I am convinced their claim is genuine, whether or not they can produce evidence to support it. Let me make it clear, once and for all, that I intend to do everything in my power to help them. I love Deborah, and always will; and one day, please God, I'll make her my wife."

There was a short pause after this firmly spoken declaration. Then James said with a rueful smile: "I'm sorry. I shouldn't have prated at such length, but I had to be sure you knew what you were doing, and that your feelings for her were not of a purely temporary nature."

"You can rest assured they are not!"

They went into the house, Charles leading the way to the book-room.

"Sit down, James." He waved him to a chair. "I believe I omitted to tell you I met Francis this afternoon and told him we'd rescued the Wyngardes and brought them here."

"Whatever possessed you to do that? You know what a rattle *he* is. He'll go straight to Howard."

"Which is precisely why I told him – though Howard probably knows already."

"He will, if his two hirelings have reported back to him."

Charles raised a quizzical eyebrow. "Coming round to my way of thinking, James?"

"You've convinced me!"

"Good!" Charles smiled, then sobered again. "Those two 'hirelings' as you call them, for want of a more suitable name, would scarcely go to Long Street. I doubt whether they would even know the identity of the man who paid them for doing their filthy work last night. The business would have been transacted through a go-between; probably the man I saw yesterday morning, following Deborah and her brother when they left Wyngarde House."

James eyed him askance. "We can scarcely go to Howard and ask him to produce him!"

"No, but Matthew has already set off on his quest to find the other two, *and* the pickpocket; and once we have *them*, a little persuasion should loosen their tongues. He's taken one of the under-footmen with him, a young springald named Robb, who apparently knows something of the stews of London. . . ."

CHAPTER EIGHT

HELEN had not missed Deborah's flushed cheeks and confused expression when the latter had joined her in the hall; it needed little perception to understand the cause. Taking the girl's hand, she led her up the wide staircase, talking gaily to give her time to regain her composure.

"We must find you something suitable to wear while your own gowns are being cleaned. Mine, I fear, would be too large for you, though Rose could make some temporary alterations; but I have a better solution."

She took Deborah into a bedchamber furnished in similar style to that which had been allotted to her, went to the heavy press and having opened it, rummaged inside for a moment. She then emerged triumphantly with a gown of cream sarsenet, embroidered with pink blossoms and true-love's knots, together with a pink satin petticoat.

"There! Is that not the prettiest thing? – And only worn once, I can vouch for that."

Thrusting it into Deborah's arms, she dived into the press once more, producing a pair of pale green silk stockings, and dainty satin shoes of the same colour, with gauze bows.

She whisked the bewildered Deborah to her own room, calling to Rose and Phoebe. The latter, Deborah learned, was to act as her own tiring-maid. She found herself seated before the toilet table, her hair brushed, combed, arranged first in one style and then another, and finally dressed in soft, loose curls through which a green satin ribbon was threaded; ceruse applied lightly to her face and neck, a touch of colour to her cheeks and lips; her temples, throat and bosom scented with jasmine water. Stockings, garters, shoes, satin petticoat, and finally the lovely gown, were put on her.

"Wonderful!" Helen exclaimed. "See—" She pushed Deborah in front of the wall mirror. "It needs something to set it off. Rose, fetch my pearl pendant necklace."

"I have my brooch," Deborah demurred.

"Wear it if you wish, but you will still need a necklace. I fancy you are not used to wearing such a low-cut bodice!" Seeing Deborah's look of doubt at her reflection, she despatched Phoebe for a green gauze collar, and when Deborah tried to express her thanks for all her kindness, shrugged it away with the remark that she had enjoyed transforming her from "a country mouse to a lady of fashion."

She said this with such a comical air that Deborah could not possibly take offence. Instead, she said lightly: "Might I ask who owns all this finery?"

"Did I not tell you? – My cousin, Anna Lambert. She is a widow, slightly older than I, who has been acting in the capacity of companion to me. Unfortunately she had to return to Surrey at the end of last month, as her father fell ill, and is like to remain there for some time – so you see, my dear, our problem is solved. You may wear Anna's clothes while you are here. She is a kind soul, and will not mind in the least, believe me!"

At this point Phoebe returned with the collar, which was then draped round Deborah's shoulders and fastened with her brooch. The pearl necklace was added, Helen declaring that the finished effect was perfection.

She then rushed away to her own room with Deborah and the maids, and the process of beautification and adornment was repeated. Her dark hair, so like her brother's, was caught up into a thick twist at the back and encircled with a string of pearls, with ringlets falling upon each side of her head. Painted, perfumed and bejewelled, she wore the gown of pale shimmering green in which Philip had seen her at the playhouse.

Supper awaited them in the dining-room. The heavy table

was covered with a snowy linen cloth on which stood dishes containing a variety of food: fish, meat, a green sallet, capons, veal pasties, tansies, tartlets and fruit. There was an abundance of wine as well, but Deborah was sensible enough to realise that if she was to keep a clear head she must not take more than a glassful or two, Charles was quick to appreciate that she was unused to it, and did not press her to drink too much.

As the meal progressed she lost her initial diffidence, regaining her natural warmth and animation and putting aside dark thoughts of Philip's injury, and the uncertain future awaiting them. The wine was mellow, the food excellent, the company gay – and Charles was there, close beside her. She was conscious of him with a new awareness, a tingling excitement that permeated the very depths of her being. Each time she met his glance, she found it hard to drag her own away.

That he approved of her transformed appearance had been clear to her from the moment she had descended to the hall in Helen's wake, and had found him and James waiting there. Taking her in to supper, he had said softly: "May I compliment you upon your appearance? You look absolutely enchanting."

With her new-found confidence Deborah sparkled, she glowed, she laughed and talked, and made the others laugh at her droll comments upon London life. James found himself revising his original opinion of her. Her wit might not possess the edge one found in more sophisticated circles, but it had a freshness and an acuteness that was decidedly engaging; and there was no denying that she was a lovely little creature. He began to understand why Charles had lost his heart to her, and to sympathise with his friend's desire to make her his wife.

Helen's contribution to the general gaiety had an almost feverish quality about it. During the past few hours she had managed to keep thoughts of Aveling at bay, but it was becoming increasingly difficult to pretend that all was well, that nothing had happened to shatter her life. Her laughter became brittle, her utterances wilder, and her eyes held a strange, hard brilliance.

She knew she was drinking more than usual, and that the wine was having an effect upon her. She no longer cared. She saw Charles glance sharply at her with a quick shake of the head. She smiled sweetly at him, and held out her glass to be refilled.

"I think you've had enough," he said quietly.

"Another glass won't – won't kill me!"

His mouth tightened. "Very well." He poured the wine for her, with the words: "That's all!"

She glared at him. "If I want more – I'll have it!"

"I've no wish for a repetition of last night," he flashed in a curt undertone.

"What do you know about last night?"

He looked her straight in the eyes. "Everything!" He then turned back to the others, leaving her staring at him in shocked surprise.

He knew!

She leaned forward, grasping his arm and giving it a little shake to capture his attention. "Who told you?"

"What?" He turned his head, frowning. "Not now, Helen. We'll discuss it in the morning."

"Why not now?" She saw that the others were looking at her enquiringly. "Why shouldn't they hear? They're our friends, aren't they?" Her voice rose. She was behaving badly. She knew it, but could not stop herself. It was as though some inner demon spurred her on. Defiantly, she drained her glass, hiccoughed, and reached for the bottle. Before Charles could prevent her, she had helped herself to the wine, slopping it on to the cloth.

"Give that to me," he said, removing the bottle from her reach. "You've had enough. It's time you were abed."

"At this hour? 'Tis scarcely past eight o'clock. Even little – little country mice do not retire so early, do they, Deb- Deborah?"

"They do – quite often," Deborah returned evenly.

"I s'pose you agree with Charles that I've – that I've drunk too much. If you want *my* opinion, *he* might be in a better humour if he'd taken a little more." She turned to Charles. "Here you are. For you – all of it!"

She dashed the contents of the glass full in his face.

For a moment he was too startled to move, then he snatched up his napkin and dabbed furiously at the rivulets of wine.

Helen began to laugh. "You look – so funny! I'll warrant that was – the last thing – you expected!"

Her laughter had a hysterical ring. Deborah hastened to her side, but James was already there.

"Come, Helen." He tried to assist her to her feet, but she shook him off, laughing and crying together.

Charles threw down the soaked napkin. "Enough of this!" He kicked his chair away, and strode round the table. "Helen, pull yourself together!"

His words had no effect.

"Leave her to me," said Deborah and, with a quick breath, slapped Helen's face hard with the flat of her hand. There was an immediate, stunned silence.

Helen, mouth agape, stared up at her and then with a sob, collapsed over the table, her face on her arms, crying as though her heart would break.

Deborah gently stroked the dark head, attempting to pacify her. She glanced up at Charles. "She's overwrought."

He nodded. "I'll send for Rose."

But Rose, it seemed, had been apprised by a footman that her ladyship needed her, and was already at the door to take charge of her mistress. Helen allowed herself to be led away, head bent, cheeks still wet with the tears that had blotched the paint on them.

"I'll go with her," Deborah murmured.

She went out into the hall, but before she could reach the stairs she became aware of a sudden commotion at the front door. It had been opened in response to a loud knocking and the footman stepped hastily aside as three men – one of them struggling in the grip of the other two – burst inside.

As Deborah watched, the captive tore himself free and

dashed forward. Immediately the younger of his two captors flung himself after him, both men crashing to the floor at Deborah's feet.

Charles and James, alerted by the noise, came out into the hall. Charles, taking in the scene, exclaimed: "Ah – Matthew! So you found him?"

The third man, a stalwart individual dabbing at a cut on his cheek, came forward, grinning.

"Yes, m'lord. That is to say, he answers to your description, but swears it wasn't him that did it. Says it's a case of mistaken identity. Robb! Get him up on his feet!"

The young footman was already hauling the luckless fellow into an upright position.

Deborah took one look at him, and gasped. "That's the man who pushed against Philip in Cheapside – the one he said must have stolen his purse!"

She turned to Charles eyes wide. "I don't understand – why is he here?"

"I sent for him." Charles surveyed the prisoner. "What have you to say for yourself now that Mistress Deborah has identified you? She recognised you at once. What is your name?"

The man swallowed. "M-Meacher."

"Well, Meacher, can you give me any reason why I should not send immediately for the constable and give you in charge?"

"No, my lord! Not that!" Meacher's expression was agonised. "I'll do anything you say, if you'll only let me go free!"

Charles regarded him with contempt. "I can promise you nothing. However, if you co-operate with me, I may reconsider the matter. Matthew, take him into the book-room. I'll join you in a moment."

"Yes, m'lord." Matthew clapped a heavy hand on Meacher's shoulder, and the man shuffled away between his two captors, utterly dejected.

"What do you intend to do with him?" Deborah asked.

"Question him concerning those two rogues who attacked

you yesterday. I have a notion he will be able to tell me where I can find them. And now, I must bid you goodnight." He led her to the foot of the stairs, and kissing the palm of her hand, folded her fingers over it, "Sweet dreams – my dear little mouse!"

He found the others waiting for him in the book-room, James occupying a chair near the table, Meacher and his guards ranged in the centre of the room. Charles seated himself behind the table, and nodded to Matthew. "Where did you run him to earth?"

" 'Tis a long story, m'lord. We went from one place to another until Robb found a man willing to tell us where he might be. One of your broad-pieces loosened his tongue. He directed us to Meacher's lodgings, over a chandler's. He wasn't there, but we found these under his mattress." He produced several empty purses from his pockets, and spread them out on the table. "I thought p'raps one of 'em might be Mr. Wyngarde's."

"More than likely. What did you do then?"

"We asked the chandler and his wife where he might be found. I'm afraid I had to part with another of your broad-pieces, m'lord, before they'd tell us he'd gone to visit his mort. So we went there. Fine, strapping wench, she was. Make two of *him*!"

Meacher scowled and glared at him beneath his ragged brows.

"Was he there?" Charles enquired, hiding a smile.

"I'd stake my life he was, but body o' me! She kept us talking so long, by the time we managed to get inside, the bird had flown. After that we searched every ale-house and tavern round Fleet Street and the Cheap. Sink me, there's not a padder or micher in the place that don't know us by now! It'd turned candle-lighting time and I was beginning to think we'd have to come back empty-handed after all, when we had a stroke of luck. You tell his lordship, Robb."

"Well, m'lord," Robb began, slightly pink round the ears at finding himself the centre of attention, "we was passing an alley when all of a sudden we heard a yell, and the next minute Meacher came bolting out – straight into me. So I grabbed him and then this old fellow appeared, saying as he'd progged his watch – and he had, too. We gave it back to him, then and there. He was all for giving Meacher in charge, but we persuaded him to let us bring him back to you."

"And here he is," Matthew concluded.

Charles looked from one grinning countenance to the other. "I'm greatly obliged to you. You've done a good day's work. Have you eaten? No, I thought not. You'd best go and have your supper . . . and – ah – Matthew, come back here when you've finished, will you?"

They went out. Meacher glanced at Charles, and measured the distance to the door.

"I shouldn't try it," Charles advised, and as Meacher scowled at him, indicated the purses lying on the table. "Which of these belongs to Mr. Wyngarde? And don't pretend you don't know who I'm referring to!"

Meacher shuffled over to the table, a sick look on his face, and after a moment's hesitation, selected a purse and handed it to Charles, who accepted it with the words, "Where's the money you took from it?"

"Haven't got it."

"Turn out your pockets."

"Won't do you any good."

Charles made as if to rise. Meacher hastily pulled out the contents of his pockets: a miscellaneous assortment of keys, grimy kerchiefs, an ivory comb, a broken pocket knife, a few coins, another purse which clinked as he dropped it on to the table, a pair of small doeskin gauntlets, a gold ring set with a sapphire, and various other items, none of which appeared to belong to him by right.

Charles took up the ring and examined it.

"Found it in the kennel," muttered Meacher.

"And the gauntlets?"

"They were lying under a bench."

"I suppose the purse was left on your doorstep?" James said, with heavy irony.

Meacher did not reply.

"A worthy collection," Charles remarked, eyeing the kerchiefs with distaste. "You can put those back in your pocket. No – not the other things. I shall have to take steps to see what can be done about returning them to their rightful owners." He opened a drawer in the table and swept them into it. Holding up Philip's purse, he went on: "This is all we need as evidence against you. You have admitted taking it, Sir James Leveson will testify to that."

"Certainly," James agreed.

Meacher's jaw dropped. He began to shake. "No, my lord! I'll do anything for you – honest I will – only don't turn me over to the constable!" His voice had risen to a thin, nasal whine. "I got away from him before. This time . . ."

"This time you won't be so fortunate. It's the Fleet and Tyburn for you!"

"*No!*" With an ear-splitting shriek Meacher flung himself upon his knees and grovelled at Charles's feet, wringing his hands, uttering broken words, and shuddering violently.

"The fellow's demented!" James exclaimed disgustedly.

"Get up off your knees and listen to me!" Charles commanded curtly. "Yesterday evening, Mr. Wyngarde and his sister were brutally attacked. Had Sir James and I not chanced to come along, Mr. Wyngarde would have been killed. I believe you are in league with the two men responsible. Tell me their names and where they can be found."

Meacher scrambled to his feet and backed away a few paces, his gaze darting from side to side, his hands clenching and unclenching.

"You want to save your skin, don't you?" said Charles insinuatingly.

Meacher licked his lips. "S'posing I did know them, and told you their names – and they found out? They'd kill me!"

"They wouldn't have the chance. You'd be under my protection. You have my word for that."

Meacher gave him a doubtful look.

Seeing his hesitation, Charles said swiftly: "You stole Mr. Wyngarde's purse because they told you to do so. You knew they'd been hired to kill him, yet you did nothing to prevent it, which means you were as responsible as they for the attempted murder. That being so, you will go to the scaffold with them."

"No!" Again Meacher cried out with fear. He cringed before Charles, words tumbling from his lips. "I never knew they meant to kill him – only that they was hired to attack him. Blount and Jackson – that's their names. Tom Blount 'n Dan Jackson. They've got lodgings next to an ale-house off Thames Street – Old Nick's."

"A fitting residence for them," murmured James.

". . . only they won't be there," Meacher finished desperately.

Charles's eyes narrowed. "They've gone into hiding, have they? Where?"

"I dunno – honest I don't! P'raps Blount's mort could tell you." He licked his lips again. "Nell Plunkett. She lodges with 'em."

Charles caught his friend's eye. "Another errand for Matthew. Ah, that's probably him now."

Matthew it was, who entered after a discreet tap on the door. Charles instructed him to take charge of Meacher and see he was safely locked up for the night in an outhouse, and then to bring him the key.

This Matthew did, with the announcement that Meacher seemed like to spend the night on his knees, having collapsed upon them once more.

"Perhaps he intends to devote the night to prayer," James commented.

"Might I ask if you managed to obtain any information from him, m'lord?" Matthew enquired.

"Yes, I did. He admitted being associated with the two runyons who were responsible for the attack, and gave their names as Tom Blount and Dan Jackson. He says they've gone into hiding, but suggests that Blount's mort, Nell Plunkett, might be persuaded to disclose their present address. She apparently lodges with them next to Old Nick's, off Thames Street."

"And you'd like me to – er – persuade her?" Matthew was grinning broadly.

Charles's answering grin was equally broad. "In your own inimitable fashion, Matthew. With Meacher under lock and key, it can wait until tomorrow. You will be needing some money . . ."

"Oh no, m'lord. I've still some left from the amount you gave me this morning. More than enough for a punk from Thames Street!"

When the door had closed behind him, James remarked, "You're fortunate to have such a devoted servant, Charles. He must be well aware of the dangers of the situation, yet he doesn't turn a hair."

"Matthew learned to take care of himself during our years in exile together, as I did. I could tell you many a tale of our misadventures."

"Doubtless!" James flashed him a smile, then sobered again. "Do you suppose Helen has recovered herself by now? Poor girl – I'd like to break Aveling's neck!"

"Would you?" Charles eyed him in some amusement. "I don't think that will be necessary. He won't trouble Helen again – and she has certainly learned her lesson as far as he is concerned."

"Thanks to the opportune arrival of his wife! I wonder how she came to hear of the *affaire*? Perhaps someone wrote to her."

Charles studied the heavy seal ring on his finger. "Or to her mother."

Something in his tone made James look at him sharply. "Her mother! Charles – are you trying to tell me it was *you* who wrote to her?"

"I decided it was time I put a spoke in Aveling's wheel."

"Od's wounds! Does Helen know?"

"Not yet."

"I wouldn't care to be in your shoes when she does."

"If she has a particle of sense she'll thank me."

James raised his brows. "She's more likely to scratch your eyes out! You'd best beware, Charles. She won't forgive you for this!"

CHAPTER NINE

WHILE Charles was drinking his morning draught, Matthew entered, his expression one of chagrin.

"My lord – Meacher has escaped. He picked the lock."

"What!" Charles stared at him in disbelief; then, setting his tankard down with rather more force than was necessary, stalked into the book-room. Unlocking the drawer in which he had placed Meacher's spoils, he turned them over swiftly. The broken knife was not there. Meacher must have scooped it up with the grimy kerchiefs and returned it, unnoticed, to his pocket.

"Fool!" Charles exclaimed forcibly. "No, not *you*, Matthew! Myself. I should have foreseen something like this."

"Do you want us to find him and bring him back?"

"I doubt if he'll be caught twice! At least I gained the information I wanted from him – the address of those two rogues. On the other hand, if they have returned to it, he'll have gone straight there to warn them."

"Not if they've gone into hiding."

"True, but I wounded one of them in the arm. He might not have been in a fit state to travel far, especially if he'd lost a lot of blood."

Matthew nodded. "I'll see what I can do, m'lord."

Deborah was standing by the window of her bedchamber, gazing down into the garden, when Phoebe knocked and entered. She returned the maid's respectful greeting, and after bathing her face and hands proceeded to dress with the latter's assistance.

Phoebe was a round, buxom little thing, full of cheerful

chatter concerning the household. His lordship, she said, had been up and about for some time, and having taken his morning draught, had gone for a ride. On his return he would escort her ladyship to morning service after breakfast. Perhaps Mistress Deborah would be accompanying them?

Deborah had forgotten it was Sunday. "I'm not sure," she replied uncertainly. "Is her ladyship dressed?"

"I shouldn't think so. She don't get up very early. Your gowns are ready for you. Will you be wearing one of them, or one of Mrs. Lambert's?"

"I think I'd better wear my own, thank you – the blue taffeta."

Deborah's thoughts were with Philip. As soon as Phoebe had finished lacing her into the gown and had arranged her hair to her satisfaction, she dismissed her and went to his room. To her surprise, Dr. Graham was at the bedside. He glanced up at her, gave her a little smiling nod, and then turned once again to his patient.

Deborah tiptoed quietly forward. "How is he, Doctor?"

"I have examined the wound. It appears to be healing well."

She looked down at her brother. Eyes half-closed, his breathing shallow, he was moving his head restlessly from side to side. His cheeks were burning with colour. Her anxious gaze lifted to the doctor's face.

"Just a touch of fever," he said gently. "He will not be himself for a day or two. The body's humours have become disturbed."

At that moment Philip's eyes opened. "Deborah. . . ." he breathed.

She bent over him. "I'm here, Philip."

His hand groped for hers. It was hot and dry. "Thirsty. . . ."

Blake, who had been assisting the doctor with the bandages, poured some water into a glass, and Deborah held it to Philip's lips. He drank it, and let his head fall back on the pillows.

His gaze alighted on the doctor. He frowned, puzzled.

Dr. Graham introduced himself, adding: "His lordship called me in to attend you."

"Lord Mulgarth," Deborah explained, seeing Philip's bewilderment increase. "He brought us here, to his house, on the night we were attacked. He and his friend, Sir James Leveson, came to our rescue. Otherwise I don't know what would have happened to us."

Philip digested this information in frowning silence. Then he moved his head in the same restless manner as before.

"We must go home, Deb. We have to catch the coach. Have you packed? We must return to Hallowden and find those papers."

Deborah glanced up at the doctor. He shook his head warningly and, addressing Philip, said: "You will have plenty of time to catch the coach. You must rest now."

Philip subsided with a sigh and closed his eyes. In a little while, he appeared to be asleep. Deborah gently disengaged her hand from his, and Dr. Graham, after a murmured word with Blake, led her out of the room, closing the door quietly behind them.

"Your brother's mind is wandering. It is bound to do so until the fever abates. Do not try to argue or reason with him – agree with whatever he says. I will call again this evening. Meanwhile, I will make up some physic to lessen the fever, and send a servant round with it." He gave her a reassuring smile. "Do not distress yourself. He has every chance of a good recovery."

With these comforting words he departed and Deborah, after a moment's thought, went to Helen's room. She found her seated at her toilet table in a pretty undress-gown, with Rose carefully arranging her hair in becoming curls and Phoebe busying herself about the room.

Deborah entered a trifle warily, not quite sure what reception she would receive after the summary manner in which she had dealt with Helen's hysterics. She need not have worried, however. The latter apparently bore her no grudge for the slap. Interspersing her conversation with comments and instructions to the maids, she complimented Deborah upon her appearance, sought her opinion upon the gown she intended to wear, and then, almost as an afterthought it seemed, said lightly that she was feeling a deal happier this morning, having enjoyed a good night's sleep.

Her gown of mulberry satin, looped up over an underskirt of silver-blue, occupied her attention for a while. She then picked up the heavy hand-mirror and stared at her pale reflection with evident displeasure.

"Ah well, there's nothing for it," she murmured, and picking up one of the little ornamental jars on the toilet table, began to apply colour deftly to her cheeks and lips, while Deborah watched, fascinated.

Helen caught her eye. "I always feel guilty when I paint myself on a Sunday. Somehow it does not seem fitting – though why I should bother about it I don't know. Everybody else does the same. There, I have finished."

She dismissed the maids. "I trust you slept well?" she enquired, with a swift glance at Deborah.

"Yes, I did . . . better than Philip, I think." She told Helen of the doctor's visit, and of her brother's fever.

Helen's eyes clouded. "Poor Philip," she murmured and then, seeing Deborah's troubled expression, pressed her hand comfortingly. "If Dr. Graham is optimistic, then you may be sure he will soon be restored to health." She rose and went over to the window. "It's a lovely morning."

Her tone was abstracted, as though she was thinking of something else. Deborah waited.

Helen said over her shoulder, "I owe you an apology for my behaviour last night, and an explanation." She turned to face Deborah. "I don't know whether you were present in Hyde Park on the morning my horse bolted and Philip risked his life to stop it?"

"Yes, I was."

"Then you probably remember my escort on that occasion – Lord Aveling." There was a slight tremor in her voice as she spoke the name.

"I remember him."

Helen sat down at the toilet table. "At that time I was in

love with him – or thought I was. I know now it was no more than infatuation. He was – is – married. I knew that, but I didn't care. Does that shock you?"

It did, but Deborah staunchly shook her head. "No." She seated herself on a stool close by, her gaze on Helen's face. "You need not tell me any more if it is painful for you. I – I understand."

"Do you?" A brief bitter smile touched Helen's lips. Looking at the girl, she saw anew her fresh, unspoilt youthfulness; and it was as though a knife turned in her heart, for in Deborah she saw herself as she had been before George Aveling had sullied her life. Her throat constricted. She rose swiftly to her feet. "Suffice it to say that the – the attachment is at an end. Shall we go down and take a little breakfast?"

She had recovered her spirits by the time Charles joined them halfway through their meal of cold meat, bread and butter and ale.

Having greeted Deborah, he eyed his sister quizzically. "I hope you are feeling better this morning?"

"Yes, thank you!" Her tone was brittle.

Deborah, sensing that they probably wished to talk to one another without a third party being present, hurriedly finished her breakfast, and pushed back her chair.

"Pray excuse me. I must go and make ready for church."

Charles rose. "You're coming with us, surely?"

He glanced enquiringly at Helen, who nodded. "Of course she is! There is no need to rush, Deborah."

"Then I will sit with Philip for a while." She went quickly out.

Charles seated himself again. "I'm glad to see you in better spirits this morning."

Helen gave him a sharp look. "I apologise for my conduct last night. I promise it will not occur again." She fiddled with her knife. "I gather you heard that Elizabeth Aveling had returned unexpectedly to London."

"I knew beforehand that she was returning," he said quietly.

She stared at him in amazement. "You *knew*? But – how?"

"Simple – I wrote to her mother, Mrs. Jennings. I felt that a letter from me would not come amiss."

She said in choking accents: "You told her about George and me?"

"I did not go into details. I merely mentioned that I thought Elizabeth ought to return to London, as her husband was amusing himself during her absence and it was time to put a stop to the affair before anyone was hurt."

"How could you do such a thing? You've made me a laughing-stock! You have shamed and humiliated me!"

"Is that not better than having you shamed and humiliated in worse fashion? Your name would have been dragged through the mud and your reputation torn to shreds had I not stepped in when I did. God knows, I had warned you. I asked you to stop seeing him. I gave you a chance to come to your senses."

"You treat me like a child!" Helen raged. "Am I to have no life of my own? Am I to be answerable to you for the rest of my days?"

"Until such time as you marry. You can always return to Grandfather if you wish."

"You'd like that, wouldn't you? You'd like to be free of me. Do you lead such an exemplary life yourself? What of Lydia Dennis?"

"That is an entirely different matter."

"Of course it is!" Her eyes flashed him a look of scathing contempt. "You're a man. *You* can keep as many mistresses as you like and no one thinks any the worse of you. As for that strumpet – from what I've heard, she's vastly free with her favours. You're a fool, Charles, if you believe her to be true to you, for she is not. Everybody knows she is cozening you. They laugh at you behind your back!"

"If by 'they' you are referring to your so-called friends to whom George introduced you, I can well imagine they would be incapable of discussing anything without reducing it to the lowest possible level. If it is of any interest to you, I have been aware for some considerable time that Lydia has been playing a double game with me, and that others are sharing her 'favours'." He paused, then added significantly: "I am no longer paying her expenses."

"You mean you have parted from her? When did this happen?"

"Recently."

Her eyes narrowed. "After you met Deborah?"

"Yes – why?" His guarded look did not escape her.

"So that's why you brought her and Philip here, instead of taking them back to their lodgings! To enable you to further your acquaintance with her, make her beholden to you, sweep her off her feet! What chance would a little innocent like Deborah have against *you*?"

Charles's face whitened. "What are you talking about?"

"Oh come! Why beat about the bush? You intend to make her your mistress, don't you? Off with the old love, and on with the new! 'Twill be an easy conquest for you – she's more than half in love with you already." Again her eyes flashed with contempt. "That you could even contemplate such a course after the manner in which you intervened in my friendship with George is utterly despicable. You say you acted as you did in order to save my good name, yet you would not hesitate to destroy hers!" She sprang to her feet. "Before you went into exile you would never have thought of doing such a thing. Now, it seems, there are no depths to which you would not sink!"

"Helen – listen to me!" he began, but she had already swept past him to the door, and was gone before he could stop her.

He did not see her again until they left the house for morning service, and had no opportunity to put things right with her.

He was waiting in the hall when she and Deborah came downstairs, the latter, at Helen's instigation, in one of Anna Lambert's cloaks, a heavy, rose-coloured silk lined with white.

"I hope we have not kept you waiting," she said anxiously.

He gave her a brief smile. "No – but we must leave at once if we are not to be late at the Palace."

"The Palace!"

"We generally attend the service in the Chapel at Whitehall," he explained. "Come – the coach is at the door."

He ushered them both outside and down the steps to where the gilded coach awaited them, a footman holding the door open; and as soon as they had settled themselves and their voluminous petticoats to their satisfaction, he climbed in and seated himself opposite them. The footman closed the door, the grooms stood back from the impatient horses, and away they went.

To Deborah, filled with excitement at the thought that she was actually going to worship in the same chapel used by His Majesty, the journey passed as in a dream. But she could not fail to note the air of constraint between Charles and Helen, and hoped they had not quarrelled.

Charles, resplendent in red silk with gold sword sash and shoulder knot, kept his gaze for the most part turned fixedly out of the window, occasionally passing some comment to which Helen replied in equally distant tones.

Deborah sighed. She had little time in which to speculate as to the cause of the estrangement, however, for they soon reached Whitehall, about which hung an air of continuous scurrying excitement – or so it seemed to Deborah, who sat on the edge of her seat, determined to miss nothing.

The coach went through the gates, past the guards, and came to a halt. The door was opened and Charles alighted, turning to hand the ladies out. A familiar voice hailed them, and the next moment James was at their side, an elegant figure in peacock blue and silver, his fair hair carefully curled and scented. Having greeted them and complimented the ladies upon their appearance, he bowed to Helen and offered her his arm. With Charles escorting Deborah, the four young people proceeded in the direction of the Chapel.

No one seeing Helen, poised and smiling, would have guessed at her inner torment as she met and acknowledged various friends and acquaintances, seemingly unaware of curious looks and pointed asides. Despite the rift between them, Charles could not but admire her outward show of composure, knowing full well how she must be hating the present ordeal.

Meanwhile, Deborah was acutely conscious of the glances that came her way. Speculative for the most part, some were warmly approving, others distinctly hostile. Clearly the gossip-mongers had been busy. She began to wish her host had chosen to attend a less important place of worship, not realising that he had deliberately brought her here in order to show them all – friends and enemies alike – that he was openly supporting her brother's claim to the Wyngarde inheritance.

It would have been false modesty on his part not to have acknowledged the fact that he had a certain amount of influence in Court circles where, apart from the special aura which his wealth and position bestowed upon him, it was well known he had the King's favour. It would never have occurred to him to use that influence on his own behalf, but for Deborah's sake he was prepared to go to any lengths.

He and Helen had a wide circle of friends, many of whom were present that morning, and Charles took care to make Deborah known to them, so that by the time she reached the doors of the Chapel she was feeling quite dazed, and convinced that she would never remember all their names.

The Chapel was rapidly filling. There was an air of expectancy, a ripple of light conversation, barely subdued even in these surroundings. The place was hot and stuffy. Most of the ladies produced little fans; Helen waved hers languidly to and fro before her face.

Deborah, seated between her and Charles, cast perplexed glances at the lively company. Used as she was to the strict Sunday observance imposed during the Interregnum, she found much to surprise her in the present congregation. Apart from a few devout worshippers in sober garb, the majority were attired in elegant silks and satins – the men with rich sword-sashes and fine lace, the women with painted faces and fashionable coiffures, white shoulders and bosoms only partly hidden by folds of lawn and muslin.

Deborah was conscious of her own plain attire beneath the borrowed cloak, which she had unfastened when she entered the close atmosphere of the Chapel, loosening the hood which framed her face so becomingly.

She felt Charles's hand beneath her elbow. The King had entered, together with his gentlemen. The congregation rose as he took his place, sauntering in his usual leisurely fashion, his tall, lean frame garbed in navy velvet, unrelieved save for the bright Garter sash and the star fastened upon the breast of his coat, his soft cravat emphasising the extreme swarthiness of his skin. His dark eyes swept over the congregation, then he sat down in his pew. With a long-drawn-out rustle and shuffle his subjects took their own seats again.

The service commenced.

The minister, gowned in white, and slightly in awe of the distinguished personage who sat listening to his every word with apparently rapt attention, preached a long-winded sermon to which few in that predominantly pleasure-loving congregation lent an ear. Even Deborah, try as she might, found her thoughts wandering. By craning her neck she caught a glimpse of the King, his black hair rippling in heavy curls over his shoulders. Nearby sat a beautiful young woman with a somewhat imperious profile. Helen, seeing her interest, whispered, "That is Mrs. Palmer – the King's mistress."

After the sermon came an anthem, with organ music and choir – both new to Deborah's ears – which she greatly enjoyed. So apparently did the King, for she could see him beating time to it.

It was refreshing to be out of doors again after the service. Deborah untied the strings of her hood and slipped it off her head, and in so doing dropped her prayer book. Before Charles could retrieve it for her someone else had done so, a gentleman in bronze and cream silk, who bowed and returned the book to her with the words: "Good morrow – *Cousin*."

She started. "Howard!"

Beside her, Charles stiffened. Instinctively he moved

closer to Deborah, a swift movement that did not escape Howard, who smiled blandly at him.

"Ah, Charles! Tedious work, listening to these flattering sermons, is it not? Francis and I have a wager concerning the King's model attentiveness to them. I contend that His Majesty never so much as hears one word of 'em, but has perfected the art of assumed concentration when all the time he is sleeping with his eyes open; Francis declares 'twould be a physical impossibility. Ah, here he is."

The gentleman in question extricated himself from the throng and came towards them, his bright eyes probing Deborah from head to foot.

"Ecod!" he exclaimed, turning to Howard. "Isn't this—?"

"Yes, Francis." Howard's voice was smooth. "Mistress Deborah Wyngarde." He looked at Deborah, his grey eyes holding hers. "Allow me to present my friend, Sir Francis Wiley, whom you may remember."

The latter bowed briefly. Deborah's acknowledgment was equally brief. She did remember him; only too well.

Howard said: "It was Francis who told me of the attack upon you and your brother. May I say how appalled I was to hear of it? I understand your brother's condition is critical, and that had it not been for Charles's timely intervention, he might have been killed."

"I cannot take all the credit," Charles said. "James was with me at the time. Between us we managed to rout the two rogues responsible for the attack, and I am pleased to say I left my mark on one of them."

"Did you indeed?" Howard looked suitably impressed. Charles, watching him closely, could detect no sign of awkwardness in his manner. "Francis tells me," Howard continued "that you have taken Mistress Deborah and her brother into your own home."

"Yes, I have, until such time as Philip has completely recovered from his injuries."

"Which I trust are not extensive," Howard murmured. He glanced swiftly from Charles to Deborah – a keen, speculative glance. Then he smiled. "Pray give your brother my condolences, Mistress Deborah. This unfortunate incident has delayed your departure from London, I fear."

"We shall return home as soon as Philip is well enough."

"For the documents? I look forward to perusing them, with a great deal of interest. Meanwhile, may I bid you good day? Good day, Charles!"

Smiling, completely at ease, he turned away, and with Sir Francis at his side, was soon swallowed up in the crowd.

CHAPTER TEN

FOR the third morning in succession Deborah awoke in the large, comfortable bed to the sound of bird calls, the muted murmur of servants moving about below, and with the sudden excited leap of the heart that answered her first waking thought . . . *'Charles'*.

She lay there, recalling his smile and the way his eyes looked into hers, and the deep, caressing cadences of his voice. She recalled, too, that he had invited her to ride out with him that morning.

Helen had questioned him abruptly. Where did he intend to go? And when he had replied vaguely that they might go through Hyde Park or along by the river, she had suggested that perhaps *she* might join them. She had said this with such a challenging air that Deborah had looked at her in surprise. Charles, with a steely glint in his eye, had retorted: "You would never be ready in time. Half the day would be gone before you had arranged your coiffure, your hat, your riding dress and everything else, to your satisfaction!"

They had been at odds with one another all day. Deborah could only hope that it would not be long before they settled their differences.

Her musings were brought to an end by the arrival of Phoebe with a ewer of hot water. Having washed, Deborah began to dress with the maid's assistance, and was soon attired in Anna Lambert's blue velvet riding-dress, a large-brimmed felt hat on her golden curls, sweeping plumes softening its somewhat mannish shape. Before going downstairs she tiptoed into Philip's darkened bedchamber, where Blake was able to inform her that after several restless hours, her brother had fallen into a quiet sleep just before dawn.

"It seems to me his fever has broken," he averred.

She bent over Philip. There was no denying the fact that he was peacefully asleep. Some natural colour had returned to his cheeks, and he no longer twisted uneasily on the pillows.

"Thank God!" she whispered.

Her face was radiant when she joined Charles in the hall, and she could scarcely wait until he had greeted her to give him the news.

His own smile deepened. "Yes, I know. I looked in upon your brother a short while ago. Now the crisis has passed, he will begin to regain his strength."

He led her out to the horses, standing in the charge of his groom, Morgan, and lifted her up into the saddle of the little brown mare he knew could be trusted to carry Deborah safely. "This," he said, "is Jenny."

They rode sedately away from the house and along the quiet streets, with Morgan following not too closely at their heels, the horses' hooves striking sharply on the cobbles. Deborah looked about her with interest. "How peaceful it is – no coaches or wagons, no noise."

Charles grinned at her. "The milkmaids will be abroad soon, then London will be stirring out of its sleep. I must admit I like this time of day, when one has the streets to one's self."

Along the Strand they went, past the great, silent mansions – silent save for the servants, already at work. Every now and then they caught a glimpse of the river, grey and smoothly flowing, untroubled as yet by the vast quantity of craft which used it during the day. Swans floated gracefully past, and a moorhen skimmed busily across the water from its nest in the reeds.

The tide was low, and on the mud flats which stretched along each side of the great waterway birds dabbled, searching for choice morsels of food. Down-river the mass of London Bridge spanned the water, solid and dark against the shimmering grey of water and sky; a grey that was suddenly irradiated with soft fingers of gold as the sun shone through the clouds.

They passed the Palace of Whitehall, watched by the King's Guards, and then to Westminster and beyond, coming eventually to the little village of Chelsea, where Charles called a halt and purchased some milk from a rosy-cheeked maid who bobbed a deferential curtsey to them.

By this time the sun had dispersed the mist and the air had lost its chill. Deborah rode beside Charles, supremely happy. He glanced at her glowing face, caressed by little tendrils of hair. Her eyes were shining. She sat her horse well, seeming to be at home in the saddle. He gave a little smile of satisfaction and turned his gaze once more to the prospect before them, of winding river, green fields and woods. A pleasant enough scene, but his eyes were searching for something else, and he soon saw what he had been looking for – two riders rapidly approaching.

Deborah had seen them too. "They must have ridden out earlier than we did," she observed. "I wonder where they have been?"

"To Richmond, or Hampton Court perhaps." Charles answered absently, his gaze fixed on the foremost rider, a half-smile on his face. "It is as I thought, Deborah. The gentleman approaching is well known to me. I should like to introduce you to him. He has already told me he would be pleased to meet you."

"Oh?" She looked with even greater interest at the horseman on his splendid black charger.

He rode, she thought, with a natural grace, and she judged him to be a tall man. His riding clothes were dark and well cut, the coat decorated with fine gold lace and gold buttons, his black hat adorned with a sweeping red plume that danced and nodded against the wide brim. He himself was exceptionally dark, his thick black curls falling to his shoulders, and he had an almost foreign look about him, with that brown skin and those brilliant black eyes. . . .

Deborah gasped with sudden shock. "It's the King!"

"It is," Charles agreed imperturbably. "Courage, Deborah! 'Tis too late to turn tail!" He swept off his hat and bowed his head. "Your Majesty!"

The King, drawing abreast of them, reined in his horse. "My lord!" His smile flashed.

"May I present to you one of Your Majesty's most devoted subjects – Mistress Deborah Wyngarde."

The dark eyes smiled into Deborah's. The smile broadened as Deborah, in a panic of confusion, bowed her head, inclining her body forward, uncertain what was expected of her.

"Pray, Mistress Deborah, do not attempt to curtsey," said that deep, pleasant voice. "So far as I know, 'tis an impossibility on horseback!"

She looked up, met those laughing eyes, and the warmth in them disarmed her completely. She felt relief, coupled with laughter, rise within her; there was no need to be frightened of this man! No need to treat him with awe. Something told her that, cynic though he might be, he yet appreciated her feelings and wished to put her at her ease.

His next words confirmed this. "Not only a devoted subject, but another early riser, I see! – Or did my Lord Mulgarth coerce you from your bed this morning?"

She dimpled at him. "Indeed no, Your Majesty! I was only too happy to be up and about on such a lovely morning."

He nodded approvingly. "The best time of the day!" He glanced across at Charles. "Are you intending to ride on, or will you return with me?"

"We will return with you, if it pleases you, sire."

"It does," said His Majesty, with a sidelong glance at Deborah.

They turned their horses and Deborah found herself between the King and Charles. Morgan and the King's attendant followed them, the horses frisking their tails, coats gleaming like satin in the sunlight.

"I hear that much has happened to you since you came to London, Mistress," said His Majesty. And as she glanced instinctively at Charles, he added: "Yes, Mulgarth has told me. I was perturbed to learn of the attack made upon you and your brother. I trust he is recovering from his injuries?"

"Oh yes, he is!" There was a note of thankfulness in her voice.

He nodded. "What will be your plans when he has fully recovered?"

"Why—" She stopped, and shot Charles an uncertain look. How much had he told the King about Philip and herself?

Charles caught the look and said swiftly: "His Majesty knows about your father, Deborah."

"I knew Lord Wyngarde in exile," said the King. "He served *my* father well; I had cause to be grateful to him for his loyalty and unstinting service. I regretted his death." The dark face was grave, and the lines that hardship and adversity had carved upon it deepened.

"Thank you, Your Majesty," Deborah murmured.

"And – your plans?"

Should she prevaricate – pretend uncertainty? The King knew Howard. As Charles had testified, the latter had become one of His Majesty's associates in exile, trusted by him and in the royal favour. So she hesitated, and then squared her chin proudly.

"We intend to return to Hallowden, where we were brought up under the guardianship of our mother's cousin, John Ryall, to find the papers which will prove our claim – Your Majesty!"

The dark eyes snapped, and the wide mouth beneath the thin black moustache, lifted at the corners. He glanced across at Charles.

"It would seem she has her father's blood in her, Mulgarth! A spirit as bold and courageous as hers deserves reward!" He smiled at Deborah. "I sincerely hope you will find your documents."

"Thank you, Your Majesty."

In this happy fashion Deborah and Charles accompanied the King to his Palace, where he bade leave of them, saying: "I hope we shall see you soon at Whitehall, Mistress Deborah. Mulgarth must bring you – and your brother also."

With a smile for her and another for his lordship, he rode

away, with his attendant close behind him, and was lost to view.

Deborah gazed after him, wonderingly. "He's so – so *easy!*"

"A little too easy, according to Chancellor Hyde! I can see you have quite lost your heart to him!"

She flushed beneath his teasing glance. "Perhaps." They rode on, and she said quietly: "You planned this, didn't you? That we should meet the King, and that you would present me to him."

He nodded. "I thought he ought to know about you and Philip." He paused. "To be more precise – he asked me."

Her eyes widened. "He *did?*"

"I often meet him on my early morning rides. Yesterday he mentioned you, and I told him your story. He had already heard something of it. Whitehall is full of gossip! He seemed interested, which prompted me to enquire whether he would care to meet you. We both agreed, incidentally, that it would be better to arrange an informal meeting and *not* one to take place in the Withdrawing-room at Whitehall, where everyone would be watching and listening and wondering." He paused, and then added, "When you do go to Whitehall you will be perfectly at ease, knowing that His Majesty is the most approachable of men; and not in fear and trembling, as you might otherwise have done."

"*When* I go to Whitehall! I do not think it very likely, Charles."

"On the contrary! Did you not hear His Majesty say I was to bring you and Philip? That was tantamount to a command!"

When they arrived in Great Queen Street he dismounted, handed his reins to Morgan, and lifted Deborah down, setting her gently on her feet. They went into the house, and at the foot of the stairs she placed a hand on his arm.

"I haven't thanked you," she said earnestly, gazing up at him. "Not just for the ride – which I enjoyed very much – but for all you have done for me – for *us*." She corrected herself hastily. Her eyes were luminous. "You have been so very kind, telling the King about us. . . ."

He took her small hand in his. "Don't you know," he replied softly, "that I would do anything for you?"

There was the sudden tap of high heels. Helen came towards them, in slippers and undress-gown, her gaze flashing from one face to the other.

"You have been a long time!" Her tone was accusing. "Wherever did you go, Charles?"

Before he could answer, Deborah said quickly, "Helen – we met the King!"

Helen raised her brows. "Lud! No wonder you look so bemused! Come – we will have breakfast, and you shall tell me all about it."

Slipping her arm about the girl's waist, she led her away, leaving Charles standing there, brows drawn together, gazing after them. Had it been his imagination, or had Deborah turned to Helen with an air of relief, as though welcoming her intervention? It was almost as though she had not wanted to hear what he had to say to her. Could it be that she distrusted his sincerity? And yet, when she had thanked him, he could have sworn that her eyes had held an expression akin to love.

There was an explanation, of course. She was very young; and fresh from some small country place where she would have led a sheltered existence. Yes, that must be it. Here, in London, everything would seem strange and overpowering to her.

He must proceed with care if he wished to win her heart – yet how difficult it would be to do so, when his every desire was to take her in his arms and make love to her!

It was mid-afternoon when Philip opened his eyes and blinked in puzzled fashion at the unfamiliar bed hangings. Turning his head he frowned at the darkened room. Where was he? He raised himself to take a better look and then fell back with a gasping groan.

What was the matter with him? He felt so weak – as though

he had no strength in his body at all. There was some constriction round his head. He put up a hand and felt the bandage . . . and then he remembered.

He lay there, eyes half-closed, recalling that sudden brutal attack in the dark alley. The last thing he had seen was Deborah struggling in the arms of one of their assailants. Where was she now? He must find her.

Slowly, carefully, he pushed himself up into a sitting position, clutching at the bed-post as the room swam before his eyes. He groaned from weakness and pain, and then lifted his head and looked about him. The window curtains were drawn, shutting out most of the light, but he could tell that it was broad day. The room itself was panelled in oak, with an ornamented ceiling, the furniture Jacobean oak, rich and heavy. There was a carpet on the floor, cushioned stools; over all an air of sombre elegance.

He looked down at the befrilled nightshirt he was wearing, which certainly did not belong to him. Where the devil was he, and whose house was this? Presumably the man who owned the house also owned the nightshirt.

With a tremendous effort he swung his legs carefully over the side of the bed and sat there for a moment before pushing himself upright. With a sudden gasp he caught at the bed-post again, and as he did so he knocked over the stool which stood beside the bed. It fell with a crash.

Almost at once the door was flung open, and someone entered the room.

"Mr. Wyngarde!"

It was Helen. He stared at her in amazement, scarcely heeding her words as she hurried towards him.

"You should not be out of bed! Let me help you."

Before he could prevent her she had pushed him down again, and he found himself lying back against the pillows with the covers being firmly tucked in round him.

He recovered his wits. "I did not expect – *you* . . ."

"I heard the crash. Thank goodness I was passing the door. You might have fallen and hurt yourself!" Righting the stool, she replaced the cushion on it. "Someone should have been with you. You should certainly not have been left alone."

He lay and looked at her. "Do you – live here?"

"Yes. It is my brother's house. He is Lord Mulgarth." She seated herself on the stool.

"Mulgarth?" he repeated, frowning. "I remember the attack, but – how did I come to be here? And where is Deborah?"

She hastened to reassure him. "She is here also. She was struck a glancing blow on the head, but the bruise is already fading. I left her resting in the garden. I expect she will be in to see you later. As to how you came to be here – I will tell you."

She did so, while he fixed his gaze on her face in rapt attention. When she had finished he lay for a while in silence.

"It would seem we owe your brother a good deal." His tone was reluctant, as though he did not find the words easy to utter. "How many days have I lain here?"

"This, sir, is the third."

"The third!" He looked away, and she studied him, her gaze compassionate as she noted his sunken cheeks, shadowed eyes, and lines of pain.

"Three days lost!" He turned to her again with a quick, impatient gesture. "We should have left for Hallowden on the day after the attack. Why, we could have found the papers by now and have returned to London with them!"

"To present Howard with a *fait accompli*?"

"You know about that?"

"Deborah told me. I believe Charles was already aware of your plans, wasn't he? I understand he was present when you and Deborah visited Howard."

His face darkened. "He was."

"Try not to worry about your lost days," she said gently. "You must resign yourself to the fact that you will have to remain here until your strength has returned."

"While all the time, Howard . . ." Philip caught back the bitter words, turning his head away. After a moment he looked up into her face once more, his expression contrite. "I am sorry if I sounded ungracious. I should not be. On the contrary, I should be happy. *You* are here. Could I wish for more?"

She returned his smile. "La, sir! I shall believe you are wandering in a fever again if you address me in such fashion!"

"Ah no—" He caught her hand and held it against his cheek. "I was never more serious in my life. You don't have to go, do you?" She had made a movement of withdrawal.

She gave him a demure look. "It is not seemly for me to be here alone with you, Mr. Wyngarde!"

"You could pretend I was your brother. After all, I am scarcely in a fit state to leap out of bed and make advances to you."

"Very well. I will sit with you for a little while – if it will not tire you."

"Indeed it will not!" He fell silent, frowning in thought, evidently turning something over in his mind. Then he said abruptly: "How is Lord Aveling?"

She withdrew her hand from his clasp. "I believe him to be in excellent health." Her tone was constrained, her expression guarded.

"What is wrong?" he asked gently.

For a moment she hesitated, then replied: "We are no longer – friends."

He was conscious of a sudden overwhelming relief. "I am glad," he said simply, adding in response to her swift, searching look: "You are too fine, too good, for such a man as he! He would have defiled you."

"You speak like some greybeard!"

"No – only as your very humble and devoted admirer."

Her gaze fell before the ardour in his. A soft flush tinged her cheeks. She attempted to smile, to answer him lightly. The words would not come. Instead, to her mortification, she felt the prick of tears in her eyes.

"You – you should not say that."

"Why not? It is true. From the moment I saw you . . ."

She stopped him with a quick repressive gesture. "You do not know me. If you did, you would not say I was – good, or fine. I would have done anything for George . . . anything. I was prepared to be his mistress. I didn't care what the rest of the world thought! I didn't give a fig for my honour or reputation. . . ."

"Because he swept you off your feet! He was determined to make you his. He used every wile, every trick he could, to win you. And once he had . . ."

"He would have won his wager!" Helen's voice cut through his, her words shocking him into silence.

He stared at her. "His – wager?"

She gave her head a little shake. "I don't know why I should have said that. I haven't told Charles. I couldn't. In any event, it seems likely he knows already. Most of the town must be aware of it." She smiled bitterly. "George had a wager, you see, that he would – would win me before the end of the m-month."

"Lecherous cur!"

"I never guessed. I thought—" She turned her head away, but not before he had glimpsed the tears on her lashes. "I thought he really loved me."

"When did you discover the truth?" His voice grated. Fury threatened to choke him. By heaven, when he was well again he would seek Aveling out and teach the blackguard a lesson!

"On the night he appeared with his wife. I overheard someone say, 'George must be furious – he's lost his wager. . . .'"

"I cannot understand why your brother allowed matters to go so far! Had *I* been in his shoes, I would have stepped in and put a stop to the affair!"

"He did. He had already warned me, but I – I wouldn't listen. So he took matters into his own hands and wrote to Elizabeth Aveling's mother, apprising her of the situation. That was why Elizabeth returned to London."

"I see." This put a different complexion on things. Philip found himself wondering whether perhaps he had been a little too hasty in his judgment of Lord Mulgarth. He saw that Helen was gazing into space, her lower lip caught between her teeth, her attitude utterly dejected. He longed to take her in his arms. Instead, he said roughly: "Don't, Helen! Don't waste your tears on Aveling. He's not worth it!"

She looked at him, her mouth trembling. "I wasn't thinking of him. I was remembering that night. The way people were watching me, whispering, laughing behind my back . . ." She broke off.

The door opened and Deborah came into the room, halting in sudden surprise. "Why, Philip – you're awake! And Helen! I didn't know you were here."

Helen rose with a hasty movement. "I – I must go." She hurried out, brushing past the astonished Deborah.

The latter turned a bewildered and somewhat accusing look upon Philip. "What have you been saying to her? She was nearly in tears."

Philip glowered at her, completely forgetting his former concern for her well-being, aware only of a feeling of irritation at her untimely intrusion.

"I did not upset her intentionally. She was – we were discussing certain matters."

"Oh?" Deborah eyed him uncertainly. "Were they connected with Lord Aveling, by any chance?"

"Yes, they were." His eyes flashed. "I'd like to break his vile neck!"

Deborah sat down on the stool vacated by Helen. "You love her, don't you?"

"Of course I do! Who could see her, and *not* love her?"

Deborah smilingly shook her head at him. "Oh, Philip!"

"I know what you're thinking." His expression was bleak. "What hope have I of winning her? What have I to offer? Even if I succeed to the title, the chances are I shall be forced to sell the house in Long Street in order to rebuild Wyngarde Court; and how I'm to keep *that* up, God knows! There'll be little enough in the coffers." He lapsed into gloomy silence.

"If Helen loved you enough," Deborah ventured, "she'd marry you regardless of your fortune – or lack of it."

"*If* she loved me!"

Deborah smoothed his pillow. "She will, Philip – in time."

CHAPTER ELEVEN

DEBORAH prepared for bed that night in happy mood. With Philip on the road to recovery, it could surely be but a question of a few days before they left for Hallowden. And had not Charles insisted upon them returning to his house to stay as long as they wished once they had found the papers? Indeed, he had suggested it would be better for her to remain in London while Philip made the journey into Hertfordshire on his own.

"It would scarcely be worth your while to go with him," he had pointed out. "He should be there and back in a couple of days."

Deborah had agreed that this would be the most sensible plan, providing Philip made no objection. She was uncomfortably aware that he had little liking for Charles and was decidedly suspicious concerning his motives. Perhaps she could ask Helen to speak to him. . . .

At this juncture, Helen herself scratched on the door and entered. She had been in pensive mood all evening, and noticeably curt with Charles. Catching Phoebe's eye as the latter busied herself about the room, she gave her a dismissive nod and the girl, bobbing a hasty curtsey, departed.

Helen glanced at Deborah. "Have you everything you need?"

"Yes, thank you." Deborah eyed her somewhat anxiously. "Is something wrong? You look so serious." She paused, then continued hesitantly: "I thought perhaps Philip might have said something to upset you. He told me he had spoken to you about – about Lord Aveling."

"Yes, he did." Helen turned away and wandered across to

the toilet table, picking up and examining various small articles, with such a preoccupied air that Deborah became more and more concerned.

"Can you not tell me what is troubling you?" she asked at last.

Helen put down the small fan she had been fidgeting with, and turned to face her. "You have grown very fond of Charles, haven't you?"

Deborah started, the tell-tale colour flooding her cheeks. "Yes, I – I suppose I have."

"And he has made it clear that he has become enamoured of *you*. But Deborah, I must warn you – he is not capable of lasting affection. He is the same as the others, seeking only a passing diversion. If you give your heart to him, it will only lead to great unhappiness for you."

Deborah put a hand to her throat, where the hammer-beat of her pulse threatened to choke her. "I have no intention . . ." she began.

Helen swept on ruthlessly. "He hasn't always been like that. His spell in exile changed him, made him hard and cynical, turning to the pursuit of pleasure above all else. Those years left their mark on him, I suppose it was only to be expected." She paused, regarding the girl's stricken expression, then went to her, placing her arm round her shoulders. "My dear, I would have given anything not to have had to say this! But it is better that you should be warned, before it is too late. Do not fall in love with Charles. You will only be deeply hurt if you do."

"Thank you for your advice." Deborah's voice trembled. "I will bear it in mind." She took a deep breath. "So you think that his kindness to me – to *us* – means nothing? That he is kind only because—" Her throat constricted. She bent her head and after a moment continued in a low tone, "—Because he seeks to place me in his debt and to win my confidence and trust and so, perhaps – my love?"

"Yes, I do."

Even as she uttered these words, Helen felt a sudden twinge of doubt, wondering whether she had said too much.

But no – of course she had not! She had acted from the best of motives: to shield Deborah from hurt.

She did not admit to herself what perhaps was nearer to the truth – that she had warned the girl against Charles purely as a means of avenging herself for what she considered to be an unwarranted interference in her own affairs. In her heart of hearts she knew he had acted rightly, but she still could not forgive him for being the direct cause of her humiliation and, womanlike, had seized upon the opportunity to retaliate.

It was only after she had left Deborah and returned to her own room that she remembered the vehement manner in which Charles had denied her accusation concerning his intentions towards the girl, and wished suddenly that she had given him the opportunity of vindicating himself before she had broached the subject with Deborah. It was too late now, she decided.

Deborah herself lay sleepless in her bed, eyes swollen with weeping, her damp kerchief clutched tightly in her hand. She knew, with an aching heart, how much she had come to love Charles. How naïve she had been not to see through him! How could she have deluded herself into believing that he loved her in return?

In the morning, pale and heavy-eyed, she was awakened by a cheerful Phoebe, who informed her that the day was warm and fine, and that she had already taken Mrs. Lambert's riding-dress out of the press for her.

Deborah's heart plummeted into her stomach. She had quite forgotten that Charles had invited her to ride with him again this morning.

"I can't go!" The words were out before she could stop them.

Phoebe gaped at her. "Can't go! Are you not well, Mistress?"

"I – I had a bad night. Please give his lordship my regrets."

She did her best to avoid Charles for the rest of the morning, or at least not to be alone with him, and found in Helen a willing ally. The latter had an appointment with her dressmaker, and took Deborah with her, together with Rose, who always accompanied her mistress on such occasions. Upon their return they learned that Charles had gone out and was not expected back until the late afternoon.

"He is probably dining with friends," Helen commented as she and Deborah sat down to their own dinner. She noted that the girl was only toying with her food and was not the least surprised when Deborah said after the meal that she felt a trifle weary, and thought she would rest in her room for a while.

Left to her own devices, Helen decided to write a letter to her grandfather. He would be interested to hear about Philip and Deborah, for he liked to be kept acquainted with the latest news. Having finished this missive, she sat for a moment in pensive thought, and then rose to her feet and made her way to Philip's room.

She found him seated in a large, comfortably cushioned elbow-chair, a blanket tucked round his knees, perusing a copy of a news-sheet which he dropped at once upon seeing her, his eyes lighting up.

"Helen!"

She crossed to his side. "How are you today, Philip?"

"Much better, now you are here."

For some absurd reason she felt a sudden stirring of the heart. "I am delighted to hear it."

He indicated a chair nearby. "Please sit down. I scarcely dared to hope you would come and talk to me again."

She seated herself with a rustle of petticoats. "Were you not expecting me?"

"You were so upset yesterday . . ."

"Ah, but that was yesterday. Today I feel – different. Reborn. Does that make sense to you?"

"Yes – if it means you have put the past behind you and are ready to face the future."

"It does."

"You don't know how glad I am to hear it. I only wish—"

"Yes?" she prompted, as he paused.

His smile was rueful. "I was about to say I wished I could

share that future with you, but I thought it might sound presumptuous."

A little smile played about the corners of her mouth. "Indeed, sir – it might!"

He sighed. "And also – foolish."

She raised her brows. "Why so?"

He lifted his hand in an expressive gesture. "Is it not obvious? You are as far out of my reach as – as the moon."

Though he spoke lightly she was quick to sense his underlying seriousness. From an early age her beauty had attracted admirers, as a candle-flame draws moths. But only once had her own feelings been engaged in return – when George Aveling had entered her life.

With him she had tasted love – or so she had thought at the time. She knew now that it had been nought but a mockery. Nevertheless, the experience had left its mark. Though she might put the past behind her, it would not be easy to forget.

She had known since their second meeting, at the playhouse, that Philip loved her, and something about the young man had touched an answering chord in herself. Had it not been for George she might have returned his love – but not yet. It was too soon.

Meanwhile, Deborah was hurrying as quickly as she could towards Fleet Street, her mother's pearl brooch pinned to the bodice of her gown. She had donned her cloak and pulled the hood over her head. It did not seem out of place, for the afternoon had become overcast, and the first spots of rain began to fall as she went along Clement's Lane. She kept her head down, not wishing to be recognised by anyone who might have seen her in company with Charles and Helen. She had a mission of some urgency to accomplish and the sooner this was done, the sooner she would be back at the house.

The streets were busy as usual, and she had to step aside more than once in order to avoid colliding with other pedestrians. Eventually she reached Fleet Street, and here she slowed her pace while her eyes searched the signs hanging out above the doors of the myriad shops and taverns, creaking and swaying slightly in the stiff breeze that had sprung up from the river, driving the rain before it.

She paused every now and again to examine those premises for which she had been seeking. A sudden gust of rain blowing into her face decided her. Taking a quick breath, she opened the door of the goldsmith's shop outside which she had been hesitating, and went boldly inside.

She emerged several minutes later, to find that it was raining harder than ever. The wheels of passing vehicles sent showers of muddy water over the unfortunate passersby. Her cloak was bespattered before she had gone more than a few steps. Doggedly, head bent, she went on her way, anxious to return to Great Queen Street as quickly as she could.

Without warning someone jostled against her, and a hand was placed hurriedly on her arm, to prevent her from losing her balance.

"Pray forgive me. I fear I was not looking where – oh!"

The voice was familiar. She looked up, eyes widening. "Why – Mr. Osborne!"

He gaped, swallowed, uncovered and bowed. "Mistress Deborah! I did not think to f-find you here. Alone. I – oh, stap me!"

She stared at him in amazement, but before she could ask him why her unexpected appearance had apparently shattered him so, another voice broke in, from behind her.

"I will be on my way, Osborne. You will see to that matter for me. Why, what the devil ails you, man?"

Mr. Osborne had, it seemed, become affected by some form of twitch – winking, nodding and jerking his head.

"The young lady!" he blurted out in agonised tones. "Mistress Deborah!"

There was a sudden silence. Deborah looked round – into the astonished face of Howard Wyngarde.

"Cousin Deborah!" His tone was sharp. Then, recovering his composure, he smiled. "What a delightful surprise. But—" he glanced about him "—you are surely not alone?"

"Yes. I had some business to attend to."

"Then please allow me to take you home. Yes, I insist! My coach is here. Oh, come—" as she demurred, "you will be soaked in this rain. Charles would never forgive me if I were to let you walk on such a day." Taking her arm, he led her to the coach. Somewhat against her will, she climbed into it and sat down, pulling her wet cloak about her, taking up as little space as she could.

With a murmured word Howard turned back to Osborne, who had rushed to open the coach door for them, and held him for a moment in swift conversation before giving instructions to the coachman and climbing in beside Deborah.

Osborne closed the door carefully and stood back, bowing to them. "Good day to you, Mistress Deborah!"

"Good day," she returned; and the last glimpse she had of him was of his sudden leap backwards as the coach wheels sprayed his legs with filthy water. Suppressing a desire to giggle, she folded her hands in her lap and, sitting bolt upright, stared out at the rain.

"May I ask how Philip does?" Howard murmured.

"He is greatly improved, thank you."

"I am glad to hear it. You will, then, shortly be leaving London for—?" He eyed her enquiringly.

"Hallowden."

"Hallowden," he repeated thoughtfully. "Would that be in the vicinity of St. Albans?"

"Yes. It is a pretty village. . . ."

The coach had halted, the street being blocked in front. Howard gave an exasperated sigh.

"One has to have the patience of a saint! These narrow streets were never intended for the traffic of today. 'Tis time Parliament formed a committee to deal with it, and seek some solution."

She returned a noncomittal answer, not wishing to be drawn into a discussion with him.

In a short while they were able to move on again, and left Fleet Street behind.

Deborah's hood had become unfastened and had slipped a little, pulling some of her hair back with it, exposing the mark of the bruise on her forehead. Howard's gaze fastened on it. He stiffened.

"When did that happen? Not – not when Philip was attacked?"

"Yes. I tried to shield him from the blows, and was struck on the head."

"I did not know you had been hurt. They did not tell me—" He broke off, compressing his lips tightly together.

"It is better now." She regarded him with some perplexity, at a loss to understand his strange attitude.

"I do not like to think of you – of any woman – suffering injury," he explained abruptly. "I am deeply sorry."

She nodded, and sought for something to say that would change the subject. "Have you known Mr. Osborne long?"

"Osborne?" He frowned, seeming to have some trouble in assembling his thoughts. "Oh – yes. He used to do a good deal of work for my father. I engaged him as my secretary on my return to England. I understand you have met him before?"

"Yes – on the coach coming to London from St. Albans."

"Indeed?" His tone was dry.

They had reached Great Queen Street. The rain had lessened, but it still dripped monotonously from roofs and trees, and the summer dust in the streets had turned to mud.

"There is no necessity for you to take me to the house," Deborah said quickly. "I can walk from here."

"Certainly not!" His eyes held amusement. "I promised I would take you home, and that I will do. Here we are!"

Barely had Howard alighted and turned to hand Deborah down, when the front door of the house was opened. Hastening quickly up the steps Deborah saw a swift movement in the hall and the next moment Charles had caught her by the arm and almost dragged her inside. She found herself looking up into his blazing eyes.

"Deborah! Where have you been? Don't you realise we had not the least notion where you were? Whatever made you venture out alone?"

STOLEN INHERITANCE 149

A cool voice drawled: "Odso! What a welcome! I did not know you kept her prisoner here, Charles."

Charles swung round, checking the oath which rose to his lips. Howard stood in the doorway, regarding him beneath his lids. Deborah looked from one to the other, conscious of the hostility that crackled in the air between them.

"Howard kindly brought me home in his coach," she faltered.

Howard smiled and strolled forward. "It was the least I could do, considering the inclemency of the weather."

Charles recovered himself. "It was extremely kind of you," he said stiffly.

"Not at all." Howard glanced at the footman, standing like a statue in the background. He lowered his voice. "It is interesting to see to what extent you have given Deborah your – ah – protection. Quite touching, in fact."

Charles's eyes flashed. "While her brother is incapacitated I am responsible for her safety, and intend to see that nothing untoward happens to her."

"Naturally," murmured Howard.

Deborah made her escape while Charles was seeing him out, colliding with Helen at the top of the stairs.

"So you are back!" the latter exclaimed. "Good heavens – you are wet through! You had best change at once." She hurried her into her room and helped her out of the sodden cloak, shaking her head over its mud-spattered condition. "I thought you were resting. Had I known you had slipped out . . ."

"I'm sorry," Deborah replied jerkily. "I had to go out on an errand. Charles settled the reckoning for us at the Gilded Peacock. I – I no longer felt happy to be in his debt, so I – I pledged my brooch."

"Oh Deborah, *no!*" Helen was appalled. "You should not have done that. There was no need—"

"I thought there was. I'm sure Philip would agree with me."

CHAPTER TWELVE

AFTER supper that evening, Charles drew Deborah aside.

"I fear I owe you an apology for my behaviour towards you this afternoon," he began. "I would never have shouted at you had I not been at my wits' end to know where you had gone."

"I thought it was time I repaid our debt to you—"

"Your *debt*?"

She did not look at him. "You paid the shot for us at our lodgings. This afternoon I went out to – to raise some money. If you will let me know how much we owe you—"

"Deborah!" His expression was aghast. "Whatever made you do such a thing? What is wrong?"

"Nothing."

"That is not true. You refused to ride with me this morning. You have scarcely spoken one word to me since." He moved closer, willing her to look at him. "You would not have acted like this yesterday. What has happened to make such a change in you? I think I have a right to know."

She felt a sudden longing to pour out her heart to him – but could not. "Perhaps I have come to my senses," she said unsteadily. "I am no longer living in a fool's paradise." And with this pronouncement, she turned and left him.

It was not until the following morning that Charles had a chance to tackle Helen, and he came straight to the point. What had she been telling Deborah to turn the girl against him?

"Nothing more than the truth!" Helen retorted. "I told her you were merely seeking a diversion, and that she would be a fool to lose her heart to you, for you would only break it. Did you suppose I would stand by and let you ruin her without doing something to prevent it? You may not have any honour left in *you*, but I have, whatever you may think to the contrary!"

"*Ruin her!*" His eyes blazed into hers. "'Od's life! That is the last thing I want to do! Helen, listen to me. I love her – I have done so ever since I first set eyes on her."

"That proves nothing! You 'loved' Lydia Dennis, until you tired of her!"

"That is an entirely different matter. I never wanted to marry Lydia!"

She stared at him. "You mean – you want to make Deborah your *wife*? For heaven's sake, why did you not say so?"

"You gave me no chance."

She put a hand to her brow. "Oh, Charles! What have I done? I was so sure I was acting for the best." She paused, flushing a little. "No, that is not true. Even then I had a feeling I was being unfair to you, but I could not stop myself. I wanted to hit back at you for the way you ended my association with George." She drew a ragged breath. "I'm sorry, Charles!"

"Has Deborah told you why she went out yesterday? In order to raise some money to repay me for settling the reckoning at the Gilded Peacock?"

She nodded unhappily. "Yes. She pledged her pearl brooch."

"Then I must recover it for her. Helen, if you want to help me, find out where she took it."

"I'll do more than that. I'll get it back!"

She was as good as her word, coming to him later in the morning with the brooch in her hand.

"Here you are! I told Deborah some tale about being short of money – a card debt I had to settle – and not being anxious to ask *your* help, had decided that the only course open to me was to sell some jewellery. She was only too happy to give me the address of the premises she visited, so I went there and managed to persuade the proprietor to part with the brooch, saying I wished to return it to its owner."

He gave her a swift hug. "You're an angel! All I have to do now is to make my peace with her. . . ."

He and Helen had a long-standing engagement that afternoon to call upon an old family friend, so Deborah kept Philip company in his room. She found him sitting by the open window, and seated herself beside him.

"Perhaps you will be strong enough to come downstairs tomorrow," she remarked.

"I hope so! Tell me what you have been doing while I have been lying up here."

She did so, describing in full her visit to the Chapel Royal, and her meeting with the King during her ride with Charles. He listened with keen interest.

"I shall look forward to being presented to him at Whitehall!" he declared, adding, "But all that will have to wait of course, until we get matters settled. I mentioned to Dr. Graham that I intended to return to Hallowden early next week, but I gathered he would prefer to keep me here for at least another ten days. I told him, however, that it was necessary for us to make the journey as soon as possible."

"As long as you are strong enough," she pointed out.

"I will be! There remains the question of raising enough money for the coach fares." Philip gave her a sidelong glance, eyes twinkling. "Maybe his lordship would oblige us with a loan, if you were to approach him? I'm sure he would refuse you nothing!"

Her brow puckered. "If you wish me to ask him I will, of course, though I would sooner you did so."

"Oh? Don't tell me you have fallen out with him?"

"No, certainly not!"

To her relief, they were interrupted at this juncture by the entrance of a footman, who informed them that Lord Wyngarde was below and desired to see Mistress Deborah.

"Howard!" Philip exclaimed in amazement. "What does *he* want?"

"I will go and see," Deborah said quickly. She had told Philip nothing as yet of her outing on the previous day, deeming it wiser to keep him in the dark for the moment.

"I will come with you," he offered, preparing to get to his feet.

"No! Stay here. I won't be long."

Howard had been shown into a small reception room off the hall. He turned as she entered, sweeping off his hat with an elegant bow. She curtseyed in return.

"I understand you wish to see me."

He smiled. "I do, indeed. You left these in the coach yesterday, thus providing me with an excuse to call upon you."

He held out a pair of gloves, and she took them, in some surprise.

"I had not realised I had forgotten them. Thank you."

"Not at all. I trust I find you well? And how is Philip?"

"Philip is well enough." The voice came from the open doorway.

Deborah spun round with a gasp. Her brother was standing there, face pale, breathing rather heavily.

Howard's eyes narrowed. "I am delighted to hear it." His gaze darted to Philip's bandaged head. "Pray sit down."

"Yes, do, Philip," Deborah urged, hastening to her brother's side. "You should not have attempted to come down those stairs alone!" She turned to Howard. "This is the first time he has left his room since the night of the attack."

"I prefer to stand." Philip's voice was hard. He looked at Howard. "What brought you here this afternoon?"

"I came to return your sister's gloves. She forgot them yesterday."

"Forgot them?" Philip's gaze flew to Deborah. "I don't understand."

"Howard brought me home yesterday in his coach – I was caught in the rain," she explained in low, hurried tones; and then, in her normal voice, "We will not detain you, Howard. It was good of you to bring my gloves yourself. You could have sent a servant."

"I chose to come myself," he said meaningly, and his eyes held hers for a moment.

She flushed and looked down, at a loss for a reply.

Howard turned to Philip. "You may be interested to know that I was down at Wyngarde Court recently. I found that the place is still structurally sound, with the exception of the east wing, which I shall rebuild. I hope it will be ready for habitation next year. The builders should soon be starting work. It will be good to be able to live in the house. My father told me so much about it."

The note of irony in his drawling voice grated upon Philip.

"I have no doubt he did," he returned curtly. "He was always jealous of my father owning the place, which doubtless explains why he vented his spite upon it when the opportunity presented itself."

Howard shrugged indifferently. "And now Fate has decreed that I, his son, should rebuild it, and live there."

"You are mistaken. You will never live there. I intend to fetch the documents next week."

"Those mythical documents!" Howard looked contemptuously amused. "Why will you not admit the truth – that they do not exist, save in your imagination; or, if they do, they are merely forgeries. Why do you not retire to your rustic retreat with good grace? You must surely know what a jesting-stock you are making of yourself, *and* of Deborah."

"We will keep my sister's name out of it, if you don't mind!"

"Certainly." Howard bowed to Deborah. "I have no wish to incur the lady's displeasure."

"I warn you, Howard, I will stand just so much of your insolence—"

"'Insolence' now, is it?" Howard laughed softly. The door had been left open. Philip and Deborah, their backs to it, did not observe as he did, that Charles and Helen had returned and were in the hall. He continued swiftly: "The boot is on the other foot. 'Tis I who have to contend with yours! I'faith, things have come to a pretty pass when country oafs come swaggering up to London, filled with presumptuous airs and graces, and pass themselves off as the sons of quality, when in reality they are nothing more than . . ."

With a stifled exclamation, Philip snatched up one of

Deborah's gloves, which she had dropped upon the table, and struck Howard across the cheek with it.

Deborah gave a cry of horror. "Philip! How could you!" She turned frantically to Howard. "He didn't mean it! You must forgive him – he is not himself."

His lips drew back in a tight smile. "There I must beg to differ. Your brother is well aware of what he is about . . . at least, I trust he is." He bowed ironically to Philip. "I shall be pleased to satisfy you, sir, as soon as it is convenient to you; when you have recovered sufficiently from your injuries to be able to wield a sword."

"At which time I shall be happy to act as a second for him," said a cold voice from the doorway.

Charles was standing there, tall and straight in gold-laced riding dress, his gaze boring into Howard. The latter bowed coolly.

"As you wish." He stooped, picked up the glove, and handed it to Deborah. He then took the other from the table and, as he gave it to her, murmured: "It is as well he did not strike me with *this* one." A remark she found totally incomprehensible.

Helen had followed Charles into the room. Howard bowed to them all.

"I will bid you *adieu*," he said; and left.

Charles closed the door. "A pretty scene! Might I ask why he called?"

"To return my gloves," Deborah replied. "I must have dropped them in his coach yesterday. He – he taunted Philip, and—" Her voice shook.

"Yes, we saw what happened."

Philip had sunk down upon a cushioned stool, his head in his hands. Helen bent over him, her expression one of concern.

"Are you not well?"

"A trifle unsteady, that is all." He glanced up at her with a wry smile. "Perhaps I would have been better advised to have remained upstairs. As it is . . ." He broke off.

Deborah had uttered a startled exclamation. She was staring down at something in her hand, something that had slipped out of the second glove.

"So that is what Howard meant," she said, and as they looked at her, held out a small crystal phial. "Perfume! He must have intended it as a gift for me."

Charles glanced at it. "A charming thought!" He then turned to Philip. "It would seem you have not wasted your time since you came downstairs."

"What would you have had me do?" Philip demanded hotly. "Take his insults without batting an eyelid?"

"He taunted you deliberately, knowing you would react in the way you did. Sooner or later it would have come to this. A duel was inevitable. You will have to have two seconds. I have already offered myself as one of them, and I'm sure James will be prepared to act as the other."

"I am indebted to you."

Helen looked from one to the other. "How can you be so rational? You talk as though it were nothing! You have said yourself, Charles, what an experienced swordsman Howard is. Did he not fight several duels in Flanders? Whereas Philip has had little or no experience!" She rounded upon her brother. "Surely there is something you could do to prevent this affair taking place?"

He gave her an odd look, struck by her unusual agitation. It occurred to him that she seemed unduly concerned for Philip's welfare.

"Would you wish me to advise Philip to write an apology?"

"You would be wasting your breath," Philip put in.

"There is something *I* should like to do," said Deborah suddenly. "I should like to return this – at once."

She held out the phial with an air of distaste, and Charles took it from her. "Certainly. I will send a man round with it."

The phial was duly delivered to the house in Long Street. Terris took it in to his master, who raised his brows when he saw it.

"Was there a note with it?"

"No, my lord." Terris retired quietly.

Howard remained standing there, the phial in his hand, staring into space. Then his face suddenly contorted. Dropping the phial on to the floor, he ground his heel into it. The fluid trickled out over the broken fragments; the heavy scent pervaded the whole room. He rang for a servant and gave orders for the pieces to be collected up, the floor cleaned.

"See that it is done at once. I am going out. When I return I do not want to find a trace of it. Do you understand?"

The man sent him a scared glance. "Yes, my lord. At once, my lord!"

A little later, Howard presented himself at a certain house near Covent Garden, where he was shown into an elegantly furnished room. A woman reclined upon a day-bed, *en déshabillée*, her abundant golden hair in careless abandon upon her smooth shoulders. She raised a white hand for his kiss. He took it, and touched it absently with his lips. She frowned.

"I was expecting someone else, Howard."

His gaze travelled over her. "Tell your maid that you are not at home to anyone else. I wish to talk with you, alone."

Her eyes glimmered with amusement. "Only that – to talk?"

He turned and crossed to the fireplace, examining his reflection in the gilt-framed mirror which hung beside it.

"That – and to take supper with you, if you will permit me."

"As you wish."

She summoned her maid and gave the necessary orders. Then she lay back and watched Howard reflectively as he smoothed an eyebrow and examined his face carefully in the mirror. He swung round.

"Lydia, do you still see James?"

She toyed with the small chicken-skin fan in her hands. "Sir James Leveson? I see him occasionally, at the play, and elsewhere. He does not come here, if that is what you want to know."

"No, he would not." His lip curled. "He is devoted to Charles. He would not dream of being disloyal to him." He flung himself down into a high-backed elbow chair. "Am I wrong in supposing that he showed a certain partiality towards you, once?"

She tapped the fan against her cheek, regarding him beneath drooping lids. "When Charles and I arrived in London, he was quite attentive." She looked down, musingly. "As you say, he is a loyal friend to Charles. He turned his attentions elsewhere."

"But he still retains a certain fondness for you?"

"Yes – I would say he does."

"It should not be difficult for you to encourage him a little."

"Why should I wish to do that?"

"For the excellent reason that he happens to be Charles's friend and confidant." His voice had hardened. "You know that my two so-called cousins are at present under Charles's protection. I learned today that they are planning to return to Hertfordshire next week. I want to know the day they choose for the journey."

She regarded him curiously. "Might I ask why?"

He smiled. "I believe you have met Deborah. A delightful little creature. Very young, very sweet; as untouched as the first blushing rosebud in June."

"How poetic!"

"She attracts me."

"Ah! You plan to seduce your untouched little rosebud? Haven't you overlooked her brother?"

"On the contrary. I have already prepared the way for his early demise." He touched his sword hilt significantly.

"A duel?"

He inclined his head, his expression sardonic.

Despite herself, she gave an involuntary shudder. "He doesn't stand a chance!"

"Do you think I am going to allow him to dispossess me – just like *that*?" He snapped his fingers. "Oh, no! For years I lived for the day when I should succeed to the title. I have no intention of relinquishing it now!"

"I have heard he has documents . . ."

"Those confounded documents!" Howard sprang to his feet, paced swiftly across the room and then turned to face her, eyes blazing with cold fire. "He will never get them. I have already set plans in motion to prevent him from doing so!"

"And if you fail, what then?"

"I have other plans, but to carry them out successfully I *must* know the day those two intend to leave London."

She frowned. "And you want *me* to obtain that information for you?"

He crossed to the day-bed and stood gazing down at her, a half-smile on his lips.

"You will not lose by it, I assure you. Indeed, you will find me most grateful." He glanced round the elegantly furnished room. "Charles made all this possible for you, did he not? It would be a pity if you were forced to give it up. If I am to believe what I hear he no longer comes here, *or* pays your expenses. That may of course be due to some indiscretion on your own part. On the other hand it could be that Charles's own attentions have strayed elsewhere: in short, to Mistress Deborah."

Her mouth tightened. "What makes you think that?"

"One has only to watch them together to be aware of the depth of his feelings for her. I must confess that part of her attraction for me lies in the fact that Charles wants her for himself. Well, what do you say? Will you help me?"

For a moment she hesitated; then nodded. "Tell me what you want me to do."

CHAPTER THIRTEEN

MATTHEW had been exceedingly busy during the past two days. Clad in old decrepit garments, he had been scouring the ale-houses and taverns in his search for Blount and Jackson and, failing them, Nell Plunkett. As a last resort he had even ventured into the dark and dangerous environs of White-friars, haunt of evil-doers of both sexes, where no law officer dared to venture without a troop of soldiers at his back.

His boldness was rewarded. In a murky tavern he ran Nell Plunkett to earth. The next morning he made his report to Charles.

"She was pointed out to me by an old cripple I'd helped when some louts were harassing him. Otherwise, I doubt if I'd 've found her. The birds who nest in *that* rookery don't peach on one another as a rule. They've a kind of thieves' honour."

"So I've heard," Charles observed. "I must congratulate you on your courage in venturing into such a den of iniquity! And I must also express my relief that you came to no harm."

"Thank you, m'lord." Matthew grinned. "As to that — well, I s'pose bed-bugs are preferable to a cut throat."

"You intrigue me! Pray elucidate."

Nothing loath, Matthew did so, explaining that in order to lull Nell Plunkett's suspicions and extract information from her, he had assumed the role of a padder on the run from the authorities.

"And did she swallow your story?" Charles enquired.

"When she found I'd a plump purse, she'd 've believed anything! She was ready enough to drink with me, and afterwards she took me back to her lodgings."

"Where you spent the night with her and the bed-bugs?"

"Aye." Matthew nodded ruefully. "'Twas worth it, though. I managed to get her to talk about Blount. Seems she's none too pleased with him, leaving her to fend for herself."

"So he and Jackson *have* gone into hiding?"

"That's right. She said they'd left London and gone into the country, to some rich gentleman's house, where no one will think of looking for them. She didn't know where the house was, or the name of the gentleman who owned it, but Blount had told her it was as much in *his* interest as theirs, for them to remain out of the clutches of the law."

"I can believe that!" Charles's tone was grim.

"D'ye think you know where they are, m'lord?" asked Matthew.

"On a certain estate in Hertfordshire, I would say, masquerading as labourers."

He said as much to James, when the latter called later in the day.

"What course of action do you propose to take?" asked James.

Charles's brows drew together. "I'm not sure. It might be worth while paying a visit to Wyngarde Court; but if I did that, Philip and Deborah would have to come with me to identify the men, and I hesitate to bring them into the business at this stage, especially as Philip has not yet recovered fully from the effects of his head wound. And that reminds me . . ."

He related the latest developments between Philip and Howard.

"'Sblood!" James exclaimed. "A duel, eh?"

"Yes; I told Philip that you and I would be pleased to act as his seconds."

"Thank you for the honour!"

"Not at all. I wonder who Howard will choose? Harry, for one. He shouldn't be difficult to trounce. He's short in the wind, and has no staying power."

"Sounds like a horse I once had!"

Charles laughed, and then sobered. "I fear it is no jesting

matter. Indeed, if it is allowed to proceed, it will be nothing short of murder."

"I agree with you. Howard has a reputation as an expert swordsman, with his experience of duelling."

"Do you remember when Philip and Deborah arrived at Long Street that morning? Howard insulted them, and Philip nearly drew on him, then and there. He rises swiftly to the bait. He hasn't learned yet to control his temper. Howard obviously took his measure at the time. You may depend upon it he deliberately incited Philip to strike him when he called here yesterday. He intends to kill him."

"To kill him!" – Neither of them had noticed that Helen had come into the room. She hurried towards them, resplendent in red silk and pearls. "Charles, you don't mean that, do you?" she demanded, her eyes wide and fearful.

James sprang to his feet and caught her hand in his. He was surprised to find that she was trembling.

"No, of course he didn't mean it!" he said reassuringly. "And remember, it is not yet certain that the duel will take place. It may all blow over. Anything can happen."

"Yes." She gave him a doubtful look, and withdrew her hand. "It's so – so unfair! Philip has never fought a duel in his life!" She swung round to face her brother. "You must stop it! Surely there is something you can do, Charles!" There was a catch in her voice.

"My dear Helen, you're asking the impossible. Philip has already made it clear that he will not apologise under any circumstances."

"Quite right," muttered James gruffly. Helen's attitude had taken him completely aback. It was natural that she would feel upset by the pending duel, but it seemed to him she was making far too much of the affair. Philip was nothing more than an acquaintance, after all . . . or was he? His brows drew together. Was it possible that during the short time the fellow had been in the house, Helen had formed an attachment for him?

His heart sank. He recalled how he had been on the point of proposing to Helen when Aveling had come upon the scene and swept her off her feet. He could remember only too well his feeling of utter helplessness; longing to intervene, but not knowing the right way to go about it without alienating Helen from him altogether. He had rejoiced when Charles had stepped in and put a stop to the affair, but had known he must proceed with care and not rush his fences. Better to let things drift for a while, and then she would turn to him again, and all would be well.

And now, all at once, there was Philip.

He was given ample opportunity of observing them together at supper, but as he could detect nothing to indicate that his suspicions were correct, his spirits began to rise again. What a fool he had been to suppose there was something between them, merely because Helen had shown undue concern for Philip's safety! All the same, it might be as well not to tarry too long before he approached her. . . .

Philip made his excuses shortly after the meal ended and retired to his bedchamber, saying he hoped they would not think him too invalidish, but he thought it prudent to take Dr. Graham's advice if by so doing he would regain his strength the quicker.

Deborah, with a murmured word, followed him from the room. James saw Charles gazing after her, his expression troubled. He had noticed during the evening that Deborah had seemed unduly quiet, but had put it down to the fact that she was worried over the outcome of the duel.

Helen, he saw, had wandered out into the garden, pleasantly cool at this hour. He immediately hurried after her.

"Helen, there is something I must say to you."

"Oh?" She gave him an abstracted look.

"I have wanted to speak to you before, but circumstances have been against it. I realise I should have approached Charles first, or your grandfather; but I don't think they would put any difficulties in my way if I were to tell them I wished to – to offer you my hand in marriage."

He had her full attention now. "You – you want to marry me?" She drew back a little.

"I love you, Helen! I would be the happiest man alive if you were to accept me."

Her expression became one of consternation. "I'm sorry, James. I wouldn't hurt your feelings for the world, but – but I've always regarded you as a friend, nothing more."

"Perhaps, if you were to think it over—"

"No, I'm sorry. I am deeply appreciative of the honour you have done me, but I fear my answer would always be the same."

Deeply disappointed, he said: "Is there someone else?"

She looked away. "No."

"It's not – Aveling, is it?"

"Lud, no!" Her gaze returned to him. "I know now that he is nothing but a philanderer, and that what I felt for him was merely infatuation. I made a fool of myself, but it's over and done with." She paused, and then added quietly, "I shall always be grateful to you for the way you stood by me." And with that, he had to be content.

It was still reasonably early when he took his leave, and feeling reluctant to go straight home, he decided to visit the piazza in Covent Garden, where he would find cards and congenial company. He felt in need of both, to assuage his hurt feelings. He had been so sure of Helen. He found the bitter dregs of disappointment hard to swallow.

Once inside the gaming-house he was hailed by a merry group of acquaintances, and with a bottle of wine at his elbow, was soon deep in play. There were several women there, painted and bedizened, in brightly-hued silks. Among them was Lydia Dennis. She watched him from across the room. He was too absorbed to notice her, she realised. She could wait. . . .

When, some hours later, James pushed back his chair and rose somewhat unsteadily to his feet, she went purposefully towards him.

"Sir James." She touched his arm, and he started, and then bowed.

"Y'r servant, Mrs. Dennis."

"I wonder—" She paused, and gave a swift glance behind

her. "I fear my escort is the worse for drink." She nodded towards the bulky figure of a middle-aged gentleman, slumped in his chair. "Would you consider it presumptuous of me to ask if you would be kind enough to accompany me to my home? The streets are so dark, and the footpads—" Her green eyes gazed entreatingly up into his own.

He bowed again, his movements bearing witness to the fact that he had imbibed rather too well during the past hours.

"Not at all! Be happy to do so."

A chair was summoned for her.

"I'll walk beside you," he said, and did so, with the link-boy lighting the way for them.

When the chairmen had set Lydia down at her door, he prepared to take his leave of her, but she would not hear of it. "No, no! You must come in for a while. I will make you some lamb's-wool. . . ."

He was never quite sure afterwards exactly what happened that night. He had a blurred memory of Lydia, in filmy undress-gown, her golden hair about her shoulders, busying herself with the sugar and spices and roasted apples, and when all was ready setting the bowl before him, leaving him to help himself. He had been unable to take his eyes from her, watching the movements of her supple body and graceful limbs. She had smiled at him and gone into her bedchamber, leaving the door invitingly open so that he could glimpse her sitting at her toilet table, brushing her hair.

He could not recall actually going into the room, but he must have done so, for he awoke to find himself lying in bed with her, her soft voice murmuring that she thought he ought to be going: it was morning.

On his way home, he mused upon the strange workings of Fate. Yesterday he had entertained the highest hopes of winning Helen, and had failed. He should have been completely cast down, yet he wasn't. Lydia had given him the consolation he needed.

He recalled that from the first moment he had met her, he had been attracted to her, but he had never attempted to take her from Charles. Now, however, it was a different matter.

She was no longer Charles's mistress. Had she not alluded to that last night, saying they had parted after a quarrel? Charles had gone, leaving her alone in the world to fend for herself as best she could.

She had raised her lovely eyes to his, helpless and appealing, awakening all his protective instincts. Perhaps, had he had all his faculties about him and had not been befuddled with wine, he might have become aware of the underlying hardness beneath the wistful entreaty, the cold calculating brain behind the seductive voice and manner.

He had not the least notion that he was being used, and would have been utterly confounded had he known that, only a few hours after he had left Lydia, Howard was shown in to her, and that *he* was the subject of their discussion.

Howard listened attentively to Lydia's account of her encounter with James, and its sequel.

"You have done well," he commented. "I must congratulate you."

"Thank you." Her tone was dry. "I think I ought to point out, however, that we have Helen Revett to thank for my — success. Had she not dashed his hopes, it is probable he would never have accepted my invitation last night."

"No-o." He rubbed his chin reflectively. "It is all to the good that he confided in you. I know I can rely on you to encourage him to do so."

She shrugged. "Naturally."

James did not go round to Great Queen Street that day. Helen, who had wondered whether he would call, was relieved when he did not. Indeed, she did not miss him unduly, for Philip came downstairs during the morning and spent the greater part of the day sitting in the garden, with Helen and Deborah for company.

Deborah was busily engaged with her sewing, having fallen in readily with Helen's suggestion that her gowns be altered to suit the new fashions. She was putting the finishing touches to the blue one when Charles joined them before supper. He commented upon the swifts circling high in the air above them.

"They'll soon be flying away," said Philip. "The summer is nearly over."

"They'll be back next year," Charles answered lightly.

Deborah glanced at him, met his gaze, and looked quickly away. Next year . . . But where would she and Philip be?

She rose abruptly, and murmuring that she thought she would go and change for supper, went quickly into the house, the blue gown lying unheeded on the grass.

Charles went after her. "Deborah – please wait!"

She drew back from him, away from his restraining hand.

"I have something of the greatest importance to tell you." His tone was urgent. "I tried to speak to you before, but you would not listen."

"And I will not listen now. No, Charles! Please let me pass."

He had put his hand on her upper arm, holding her so that she could not move. His eyes searched her face.

"What have I done that you should treat me in this way? You said something the other day about living in a fool's paradise; but you must know that my feelings for you—"

"Your feelings do not concern me in the least! Were I free to do so, I should leave this house *now* – at once! The sooner I can do that, the happier I shall be!" Wrenching herself free, she sped away.

Charles stood there for a moment, as though turned to stone. Then, drawing a deep breath, he strode upstairs to his bedchamber, from which he emerged some time later attired for the evening in doublet and breeches of emerald green silk, his hat tucked beneath his arm. He met Helen in the hall.

Without giving her time to speak, he said curtly: "I am going out. I shall be late back. Don't wait up for me."

Her eyes widened. "This is a sudden decision on your part, isn't it?"

"Perhaps. Pray convey my apologies to the others."

"I will. Might I ask where you are going?"

He clapped his hat on his head. "The piazza, the Groom Porter's, I don't know – I haven't made up my mind yet. Goodnight!"

Helen sighed, and went slowly up the stairs, heavy-hearted. She knew instinctively what had happened – he had tried to put things right between himself and Deborah, and had not succeeded. Indeed, he had probably made the situation worse.

"And it's all my fault," she thought wretchedly. "Had I not warned Deborah against him, all would now be well."

Deborah herself was quiet and withdrawn during supper. Helen did her best to include her in the conversation, but as the meal proceeded it was inevitable that she and Philip should address most of their remarks to each other, leaving Deborah to her thoughts. When they rose from the table she pleaded a headache, and retired to her room. Philip stared after her, a slight frown between his brows; but he made no comment.

Helen led the way into the drawing-room, halting beside a small table.

"Would you care to play picquet with me?"

He smiled. "I should – very much."

They began to play, time passing almost unnoticed. The servants had long since lit the candles before Helen sat back with a little laugh, informing him that he was far too good for her and that she feared she had played badly.

"Perhaps that was because your thoughts were elsewhere," Philip said. "Is something troubling you?"

She hesitated and then, meeting his steady gaze, began a halting explanation, finishing despairingly: "The blame is mine! If only I had kept quiet. . . ." She rose quickly to her feet and turned away, but not before he had seen the rush of tears to her eyes.

He immediately got up and put a hand on her arm. "Don't distress yourself, Helen, please! If your brother really loves Deborah, I'm sure he will find some way to make her believe him. He is not exactly without experience in such matters." He gave a wry smile. "I must confess there was a time when I found it hard to believe that his intentions towards her were strictly honourable."

She dabbed at her eyes with a fine lawn kerchief. "It seems we both misjudged him."

"You must not cry." He took the kerchief from her, and gently wiped away a tear.

For a moment they regarded each other in silence. Then, without warning, he bent his head and kissed her, not entirely satisfactorily, for she, taken by surprise, moved her head so that his lips merely brushed the corner of her mouth.

He drew back. "I – I am sorry. I had no right to do that. Pray forgive me." He turned away, and began to gather up the picquet cards.

She watched him, her heart beating quickly, willing him to look at her, to take her in his arms and kiss her again.

But, "It is late," he said, frowning down at the cards. "I was thinking – tomorrow is Sunday. Instead of accompanying you and your brother, Deborah and I could attend morning service elsewhere. It would make the situation easier."

"As you wish." Her words were barely audible. Clearly he had no intention of kissing her again; and had probably only done so in the first instance because he had been moved by her tears, not for any other reason.

She moved towards the door. "You are right – it is late. I will bid you goodnight, Philip."

She had gone before he could open the door for her. He sank down into a chair, staring bleakly into space. She would never know how much it had cost him to turn from her, when with every fibre of his being he longed to crush her against him, to cover her face with kisses; but he knew he must put all thoughts of love from him. Had he not said she was as far beyond his reach as the moon?

Dawn was breaking when Charles left the gaming-house. He hailed a chair, and was soon being borne homeward by the two stalwart chairmen. Lost in abstraction, he did not at first notice the route they were taking, until he suddenly caught sight of a familiar figure emerging from an equally familiar house – a house to which he himself had been a frequent visitor not so long ago.

A startled oath sprang to his lips. Could it be that *James* was now Lydia's lover? It was the last thing he had suspected. James was in love with Helen, wasn't he? He would never look at another woman while his heart was given to her. Unless they had quarrelled.

He broached the subject with Helen on their way by coach to the Chapel Royal later that morning.

She looked surprised. "Quarrelled? Why should you think that?" She paused, biting her lip, then added: "Has he told you he proposed to me, and I refused him?"

"Ah!" said Charles, as understanding dawned. "That explains it. Er – why he hasn't called."

Philip and Deborah attended St. Clement Dane's church on foot, having declined Charles's invitation to accompany him and Helen to the Chapel Royal. It was time, Philip declared, that he learned to use his legs again – and no one argued with him, or attempted to persuade him to change his mind. A feeling of constraint hung over them all like a dark cloud, and might have continued to do so indefinitely had not something totally unforeseen occurred.

They were finishing dinner next day, when a footman entered to announce that a person calling himself Luke Catchpole wished to see Mr. Wyngarde urgently.

"Luke!" cried Deborah, paling a little. She met her brother's startled glance. "Something is wrong at Hallowden!"

At Charles's command, Luke was shown in to them; a large, ruddy-faced countryman, hat in hand, travel-stained and weary after his long ride.

"My, but 'tis a big place, this here London," he remarked, having greeted them all with a respectful bow and a beaming smile. "I were beginning to doubt I'd ever find you, Mr. Wyngarde."

"You went to the Gilded Peacock first, I suppose?"

"Oh no, sir. We'd heard you weren't there no longer."

"Who told you that?" asked Deborah in surprise, adding contritely: "I had intended to write to let you know what had happened to us."

"'Twas Mr. Oliver told us about the attack those men

made on you, and how you was saved by Lord Mulgarth and brought here."

"Mr. – Oliver? Who is *he*?"

"Ah! I thought you might not've heard of him, for all his fine words, and making out he was your lawyer."

"I think you had best take a chair, Luke," Charles interposed at this juncture. "And perhaps a tankard of ale—?" He nodded to the waiting footman, who hastened to fetch it.

Thus fortified, Luke recounted his tale.

Mr. Oliver, he said, had called during the previous week, saying he was a London lawyer, sent especially by Mr. Wyngarde to collect certain important documents that would establish his claim to the title and estate.

"He said his lordship, your father, had died in exile. We was mortal sorry to hear it." Luke's normally cheerful face saddened. Heaving a sigh, he continued: "We told him we couldn't hand over anything, not without your orders in writing. He didn't like that much." He grinned. "You should've heard all the terrible long words he used, trying to make us do what he wanted, and threatening us with the law if we didn't."

Philip snorted. "What did the fellow look like?"

Luke scratched his greying head. "Shorter than *you*, Mr. Wyngarde, and a trifle on the plump side. His suit was of good broadcloth, and his linen of good quality, too. Ar – and he smelt of perfume. Mattie said 'twas heliotrope, or some such."

Deborah uttered an exclamation. "Mr. Osborne uses heliotrope perfume! And *he's* plump. . . ."

"Osborne," echoed Charles, eyes narrowing.

"Howard's secretary," Philip said. "Who else could it have been? I'm only surprised Howard didn't send his bully-boys to Hallowden instead."

"Ar, but he did!" exclaimed Luke. "Leastways, two men forced their way in."

He went on to explain that a neighbour's barn had caught fire and while he and the other men at Hallowden were helping to fight the blaze, two ruffians had broken into the house, tied up Mattie and the maidservants and ransacked the place. Doubtless they had been responsible for starting the fire, in order to get the men out of the way.

"We thought at first they was just after money and valuables, for they did take some silver spoons and a few other things; but then we found they'd broken open drawers and stolen a lot of papers – bills and suchlike – and we realised they'd come for the documents. Not being able to read, they'd taken the other stuff instead."

Philip had been listening with strained attention. "They didn't find the documents?"

"Bless you, no sir! After Mr. Oliver's visit, Mattie took the box they was in and hid it under the floorboards in Mr. Ryall's old room. You remember, sir, there was always a hiding-place there?"

"Yes, I remember. So you've brought them with you today?"

Again Luke scratched his head, a rueful look on his broad countenance. "No, I haven't, sir. Mattie, she wouldn't let me. Said they'd be safer where they was until you came home again. She thought, y'see, that those knaves might set upon me on the way and take the box by force. But I thought I ought to come, to let you know what's been happening."

"Quite right, Luke." Philip spoke abstractedly.

Luke glanced from him to Deborah. "Would it be Mr. *Howard* Wyngarde who's responsible for what's happened?"

"Yes, it would." Deborah gave him a brief account of the way in which matters stood between Philip and their cousin.

Luke's brow darkened. "'Swounds! What right has he to the title? 'Tis Mr. Wyngarde here, who's the true heir! But does he need the documents to prove it? Mattie and I could speak for you both. Haven't we known you all your lives?"

Philip roused himself from his brown study. "I fear that wouldn't be sufficient. Didn't you once swear on oath that we were dead?"

"Only to put those whoreson Roundheads off the scent!"

Philip turned to Charles. "Luke's news has decided me. Deborah and I will return to Hallowden tomorrow."

"Of course. And you will travel in my coach. Much more comfortable than the public stage." Charles's tone brooked no argument. He was perfectly well aware of Philip's lack of funds, and, which was perhaps more important, knew how much it would hurt the young man's pride to have to ask for a loan. By offering the use of his travelling coach, he had at least saved him that.

Helen, who so far had remained silent, now addressed Philip. "I presume you will be returning to London on the day after tomorrow? That being so, there is surely no need for Deborah to accompany you, is there?"

He glanced at Deborah, who gave a quick little shake of the head and, acutely conscious of Charles's intent gaze, said: "I would rather go home with you and remain there until everything is settled."

After supper that evening, Charles came up to her. "Come – I have something of yours I wish to return to you."

Without waiting for an answer, he took her arm and led her into the bookroom. Having closed the door, he crossed to the table and unlocked one of the drawers.

"Here it is, Deborah."

She gasped. "My brooch! How did you get it back?"

"I asked Helen to do so for me."

She took it. "Then – then that tale she told me about needing money, and wanting to sell her earrings, was just—"

"A pretext," he finished for her, adding as she pinned the brooch to her bodice: "And I trust that this is the end of the matter!"

"Very well." Her tone was stiff. "If that is all—"

"Not – quite." He moved nearer. "Do you recall that morning in St. James's Park, when we first met? Ah, I see you do! The crowds, pushing and jostling against us. You would have been swept off your feet had I not held you, like this." His arm went round her shoulders. "All those people, Deborah, and I saw only you." His voice had softened. "I held you here, against my heart, and from that moment I knew it would beat for you alone. Until I found you, I did not know what love meant, and then – oh, my darling! – I wanted to take you up in my arms and carry you away!"

His eyes held hers, with that compelling look that turned her heart over. There was a strange, fluttery feeling in her throat. For a moment she swayed towards him; then all at once recalled Helen's warning.

She took a quivering breath. "That – that sounds very plausible, but very *practised*, too. I am sure you must have said it with good effect before, but this time—"

His eyes burned suddenly. "What do you mean?"

"That I don't choose to believe you! I – I have no intention of being swept off my feet. You are merely wasting your time."

"Am I?" There was a look in his eye that made her stomach take a swift downward plunge. "If you refuse to believe my words, perhaps *this* will convince you!"

Before she had the remotest idea of his intentions, he had crushed her against him with cruel force, his hand cupped her face, turning it up to his, and his mouth sank over hers. His kiss, savage and demanding, drove all resistance from her; left her half-fainting and gasping for breath.

The mist cleared from his vision. His gaze searched her face: her lashes fluttered on her wet cheeks. There was a drop of blood on her bruised lips.

"Oh, Deborah!" His voice was charged with emotion.

He began to cover her face with little, burning kisses; and then his lips sought hers once more, kissing them over and over again, seeking, and eventually winning, her response. Her arms went round his neck. She was lost in his embrace, lost to all else, borne upon this swift, surging tide of emotion that carried her far, far beyond anything she had ever known, held fast in his arms in sweet surrender.

Charles looked down at her and gently brushed away a loose strand of her hair. She let her head fall against his shoulder, scarcely knowing what she did for the wild tumult within her. She was vaguely aware of his voice murmuring tender endearments, of his hand caressing her, of the hard, masculine strength of his body.

Raising her head, she looked up into his face. For one unguarded moment her eyes met his, and he read in them all he yearned to know.

"My love!" He bent his head to hers again.

"No!" In sudden panic she pushed herself away from him. "Let me go! Please—"

With a strangled sob, she turned and fled, not stopping until she had gained the refuge of her bedchamber. Sinking down on the stool before the toilet table, she sought to still her trembling agitation, and marshal her scattered thoughts.

She could still feel the tight band of his arm around her, the touch of his hand upon her breast. Her heart leapt within her, the hot blood flooded her cheeks. She hid her face in her hands, but could not shut out the memory of his passionate kisses, and of her own response to them.

It was clear to her now that he had previously held that passion in check and that she, by her repeated refusals to listen to his declaration of love and by the way she had spurned him, had inflamed him to a point beyond which he could no longer restrain his feelings for her.

She had fled from him not because she had been repulsed by his ardour, but because she had become overwhelmingly conscious of her own awakening emotions, and of the feeling that she was being swept out of her depth.

She knew without doubt that she loved him; that, despite Helen's warning, her heart was his, for ever.

Helen found Charles seated at the book-room table, deep in thought. He roused himself as she approached.

"I have just sent Matthew round with a letter for James. I thought it might interest him to know that his rival is leaving tomorrow." He quirked an eyebrow at her.

"His rival, indeed!" She seated herself with a swish of silken petticoats, chin at a combative angle.

He grinned. "Can you deny it?"

"Would you believe me, if I did?"

"No. I think you are in love with Philip Wyngarde. I am certain *he* is in love with *you*."

She grimaced. "Is he? I thought so too, but now I am not so sure. For some reason his devotion appears to have waned."

"Whilst yours has grown?" His tone was gentle. "My poor Helen! It is not lack of ardour that prevents him from paying his addresses to you, but pride. You are a rich woman. He is comparatively poor."

"But that is ridiculous! As though it matters!"

"To him it does."

"Perhaps he will feel differently about the situation once he has successfully claimed his rights. Which reminds me. I believe I told you I have had a letter from Grandfather, saying he would welcome a visit from me; so I thought it might be a good idea if I were to travel with Philip and Deborah as far as Barnet. Grandfather will give us dinner, and then they can go on to Hallowden while I stay overnight. . . ."

"Leaving Philip to pick you up on his return journey next day?" Charles's eyes lit with laughter. "Why not? You will, I trust, have Rose to chaperon you?"

"Of course," she retorted, adding with an enquiring glance at him, "You seem to be in excellent humour tonight. Have you succeeded at last in making your peace with Deborah?"

He nodded, smiling. "Yes, I think I may say I have."

CHAPTER FOURTEEN

CHARLES handed Deborah up into the coach, waited while she settled herself and then, with one foot on the step, leaned forward, took her hand and bore it to his lips. "Goodbye, my darling – for just a little while!"

He then stepped aside to allow the others to climb in, and in a few moments they were away. He went back into the house, which seemed suddenly unbearably empty. His thoughts returned to the conversation he had had with the King, whom he had encountered earlier that morning, while riding. His Majesty, who kept well abreast of Court gossip, had asked him for the latest news concerning the Wyngarde affair.

"So that's the way the wind blows," he had commented, when Charles had recounted Luke's tale. "I trust no one outside your household is aware that Mr. Wyngarde and his captivating sister are journeying home today? I should not care to think of them running into danger."

"Sir James Leveson knows, but he is no friend of Howard Wyngarde's."

"Maybe not, but I hear on good authority that a certain lady is – shall we say – on close terms with both gentlemen." His Majesty had shot Charles a sidelong glance. "Make of that what you will."

Charles did – and found the answer disturbing.

Matthew had brought back a note from James on the previous evening, regretting that he could not call round, as he had a prior engagement. Could it have been with Lydia? Had he confided the news to her that the Wyngardes were returning to Hallowden? And had *she* sent word to Howard?

There was but one way to discover the truth. Charles ordered his horse to be saddled again.

James was still in bed, and none too pleased at being hauled out of it.

"Lydia in collusion with Howard? — I don't know what you're talking about," he spluttered. "In any event, how should *I* know what she does?"

"James, I haven't time to beat about the bush," Charles declared. "I know you and Lydia have an understanding, so don't try to deny it. I no longer care how she conducts herself, so that aspect of the situation doesn't bother me. What *does*, however, is the fact that she may have informed Howard that Philip and Deborah were leaving this morning. Did you tell her?"

"Well, I — I may have done so." James was finding it difficult to meet Charles's eye. "In fact, yes, I think I did."

Charles swore beneath his breath and turned for the door.

James put out a restraining hand. "What are you going to do?"

"Call at Wyngarde House. If Howard is at home, there's no need for alarm. If he's left for the country. . . ."

"Let me come with you! I feel — well, partly responsible—"

"Get dressed and go round to Great Queen Street. If I'm not back, wait for me there!"

The footman who answered Charles's knock at Wyngarde House informed him that Lord Wyngarde was away from home. No, he couldn't say where his lordship had gone, nor when he would return.

Charles produced a crown from his pocket. Had his lordship perhaps left that morning for Wyngarde Court? The man stared at the coin, hesitated, and then nodded. "Good!" said Charles, tossed him the crown, and strode back to his horse.

He found James waiting for him upon his return.

"I've been thinking," the latter announced. "If what you say is true, and Lydia and Howard *are* plotting together, then she — she was merely using me as a — a cat's paw."

"Exactly!" said Charles drily.

"Oh God! What a dolt I've been! How did you find out about us?"

"I saw you leaving her address one morning, early. Are you ready?"

James gaped at him. "Ready for what?"

"There's only one thing to do – ride after the coach. With luck, we should catch up with it before Howard can put his plan into action. He's a desperate man, and I believe he'd go to any lengths to stop Philip. Remember, he has already tried once to have him killed!"

Welford House, residence of the old Marquis, stood in extensive grounds near the village of Barnet. As the coach bowled along the avenue towards the red-brick Tudor mansion, Deborah expressed the hope that Helen would not incur her grandfather's displeasure by bringing two uninvited guests with her.

Helen swiftly reassured her. "He will be only too happy to entertain you. He has so few visitors, these days." And indeed the Marquis welcomed them warmly, telling them that he had met their father more than once in the old days.

When they had gone, Helen said casually, "What did you think of Philip?"

Her grandfather chuckled. "Ha! Set your sights on him, have you? Well, you could do worse. He seems to have a good head on his shoulders. Tell me more about him."

Nothing loath, she did so, while he listened indulgently. All at once, she broke off. "There are some horsemen coming up the avenue." She went to the window. "Good heavens – it's Charles and James!"

As soon as the new arrivals had been shown in and had exchanged courtesies with the Marquis, she demanded to know why they had come.

Charles glanced at her. "When did Philip and Deborah leave?"

"About a quarter of an hour ago."

"The devil! We'd have been here sooner had my horse not

cast a shoe. We wasted time finding a stithy. Come, James – we'd best be off."

"Not before you explain what this is all about!" Helen demurred.

He did so, as swiftly as he could, finishing: "It's my belief Howard intends to abduct them and take them to Wyngarde Court. We'll go there first. If we draw a blank, we'll ride on to Hallowden."

Away they went, with Matthew and Robb at their heels. Helen watched them out of sight, then turned to the Marquis.

"Grandfather, I must go after them! I can't remain here, not knowing what is happening. I'll have a horse saddled. . . ."

"I'll not have you careering about the countryside. I have a better idea. We'll *both* go – in my coach."

Unaware of pending danger, Philip and Deborah were travelling happily on their way when, with shocking suddenness, came the sound of a pistol shot, followed by a shouted command. The coach lurched to a standstill, and was immediately surrounded by a body of armed men. Danby was ordered off his box, Luke and the two grooms Charles had sent as escort told to dismount. All four were marched away.

Deborah clutched at Philip's arm. "Is it – highwaymen?"

"'Tis more likely to be our *cousin's* men!" Philip clapped a hand to his sword, but before he could draw it the door was wrenched open and a dark-visaged ruffian appeared, brandishing a pistol.

"Oh no you don't, cully," he exclaimed roughly. "I'll have that! Unless you want a bullet in yer!"

With the greatest reluctance, Philip relinquished his weapon. The man took it, and then spoke to someone standing behind him. "You'd better make sure they're the right ones, sir. His lordship won't like it if we make a mistake."

He stood back, revealing the familiar figure of Mr. Osborne, whose gaze flickered nervously over Philip and Deborah. He gave a little nod.

"Yes. They are the – the right people. Let's go, shall we?"

"Where are you taking us?" Philip demanded.

"To Wyngarde Court." Osborne hesitated, and then added in a hurried undertone, "I beg of you, sir, comply with his lordship's wishes for your own sake and that of – of Mistress Deborah!" He withdrew. The door was slammed, and the coach started off with its escort of armed men.

"What do you suppose Howard intends to do with us?" Deborah's voice shook a little.

"He'll probably keep us under lock and key until he gets the documents. Having failed twice before to obtain them, he doubtless means to try another method."

Having arrived at the house, they were whisked quickly inside and taken to a large, sparsely-furnished room at the back of the Great Hall, where Howard was sitting at the head of a long draw table, a bottle and glasses before him.

He rose to his feet, a trace of malice in his smile. "Welcome to Wyngarde Court. I trust you had a comfortable journey. No difficulties, Osborne?"

"Er, no, m'lord!" Osborne came forward, looking none too happy.

"Good!" Howard's gaze returned to Deborah and Philip. "Do, pray, make yourselves at home."

Deborah glanced about her, at the old dark panelling, scarred by the pikes of the Roundhead soldiers who had searched the place for her father, at the low, deep-set windows which looked out upon a tangle of garden, the massive fireplace with its carved family crest. There was a door in the panelling, which probably opened into another room. Philip would know. . . .

Howard was by her side. "A glass of canary, Cousin Deborah?" He slipped a hand familiarly beneath her arm, and led her towards the table. His gaze went over her in equally familiar fashion. "'Tis time, I think, that we became better acquainted. Later, perhaps . . ."

His voice, low-pitched, did not carry to Philip's ears. Nevertheless, the latter saw his sister's discomfiture.

"Say what you have to say, and let's be done with it!" he exclaimed.

"Very well. Please be seated." Howard indicated the two chairs which had been set for them, one on each side of the table, and having poured the wine nodded to Osborne, who brought him a flat wooden box from a side table, taking from it two sheets of stiff paper which he handed to Howard. He then fetched a silver standish, which he set before Philip.

"I have brought you here," Howard said, "for the purpose of putting your signature to a couple of documents which have been drawn up for me." He tapped the top paper. "This is a renunciation of your claim, together with a declaration that all records purporting to support it are forgeries. The other is a letter to your housekeeper, requesting her to hand to the bearer the papers in question."

He handed the sheets to Philip, who perused them and then tossed them contemptuously down. "Surely you don't expect me to sign away my birthright!"

Howard leaned back in his chair, his hard gaze never leaving Philip's face. "I think you will, when you have considered the alternative."

"Would you have me beaten senseless again? I've no doubt Blount and Jackson are within call, should you require their services!"

"So you have learned their names, have you?" Howard shrugged. "Why should I wish to resort to violence when other – and more agreeable – forms of persuasion present themselves?"

"What, for instance?"

Howard switched his gaze deliberately to Deborah. "Can you not guess?"

Philip's chair crashed to the floor as he sprang to his feet. "Lay one finger on Deborah, and I'll kill you!"

Howard looked amused. "So you would defend your sister's honour to the death, would you?"

With a furious oath, Philip flung himself at Howard, but before he could reach him, a pair of hands gripped him round the arms, pinioning them to his sides. He was dragged away, struggling to free himself, conscious of Howard's derisive amusement and Deborah's shocked, pale face.

At a sign from Howard he was released, and turned to look at his captor. It was the same dark-visaged ruffian who had taken his sword.

"Which one are you?" he demanded, panting. "Blount, or Jackson?"

"This is Jackson," Howard said. "'Twas fortunate he was within earshot. Otherwise I might have been forced to run you through in self-defence."

"You coward!" Deborah cried. "Is there nothing you would not do in order to obtain your own ends?"

"Nothing, my dear." He looked at Philip. "Well?"

Philip's mouth tightened. "If I sign your damned papers, will you give me your word that you will set us both free?"

"But of course!" Howard's tone was smooth.

"He lies!" Osborne stepped forward, breathing quickly. "He has no intention of setting you free. He means to kill you, Mr. Wyngarde, and then—"

Howard was on his feet, expression murderous. "Hold your tongue! I have given my word—"

"But you have no intention of keeping it!" Osborne faced him with the courage of desperation. "I know your ways, my lord! You'd cheat and lie and – and worse . . ."

"I warn you – have a care what you say!"

"I have kept quiet for too long. Cheating your own kind is one thing, but ruining the lives of innocent people is another!"

"If what you say is true," Philip interposed quickly, "then these—" he picked up the papers "—are worthless!" He tore them across, and then across again.

Howard looked at him, a curious glint in his eye. "You may have cause to regret your ill-judged action. Jackson, fetch this gentleman's sword!"

Deborah's knees turned to water. "What do you intend to do?"

He smiled. "You will doubtless remember that your brother challenged me to a duel—"

"No!" White to the lips, she stumbled to her feet. "Do not, I beg you, force him to fight you!"

"He leaves me with no alternative. There is your sword, cousin. I trust you know how to use it!"

Philip looked at the weapon which Jackson had placed on the table. "Of course."

He removed his coat. Howard followed suit, his movements purposeful. He was very sure of himself, very sure of what the outcome would be.

With sinking heart, Deborah watched as the two men faced one another, saluted, and then engaged. It was plain from the start that Philip was no match for his cousin. Time and again Howard's blade flashed past his guard, and only quick footwork on Philip's part saved him from injury.

The inevitable happened. Howard lunged, his sword passing easily beneath Philip's and finding its target. Philip jerked back with a smothered cry, his sleeve slashed, blood oozing from the wound in his arm.

Howard, sword poised, waited with a faint smile on his lips, sensing victory. They had all been so intent upon the duel that none of them had heard the sudden sounds of discord from the Great Hall until all at once the door burst open, and one of Howard's men rushed in.

"M'lord! There's someone here, insisting on seeing you!"

He was plucked unceremoniously out of the way. "Stand aside, fellow. I have business with your master." It was Charles, his gaze going swiftly over the scene. For an instant his eyes met Deborah's with a look of reassurance, then he addressed Howard.

"It seems I have arrived in the nick of time." He strolled forward, pulling off his gauntlets. "As you have disabled your opponent, I trust you will not object if *I* take his place?"

"*You?*" Howard's expression was one of suppressed fury. "Nothing would please me more!"

Osborne had taken charge of Philip, helping him over to a chair. With his assistance, Deborah bound the wound with a large clean kerchief.

Charles tossed his hat down on to the table, and after removing his baldrick took off his riding coat, his movements calm and unhurried. Catching Deborah's anxious gaze upon him, he smiled at her.

"I've left James in charge in the Great Hall with a couple of my men. And you've no need to worry concerning the fate of Luke and the others. We found them trussed up behind a hedge, shouting for help. It shouldn't take them long to make their way here. Did you say something, Howard?"

Howard's nostrils flared. He shot a malevolent look at Osborne, who was pouring wine for Philip. "I thought I told you to make sure they were gagged?"

Osborne gazed back at him defiantly. "Very likely you did, m'lord. It must have slipped my mind."

Having completed his preparations, Charles stepped forward. "Ready, Howard?"

They fought in grim silence, and those who watched were also silent, so that the only sounds in the room were the clash of the blades, the snatched breaths, the scrape and slither of feet shifting over the bare boards – and this time Howard did not smile. Charles was swift and sure and deadly. His concentration never wavered; his wrist appeared to be an extension of the finely-tempered steel, untiring, supple, always ready to parry a thrust, to make a swift riposte.

That his opponent was a fine swordsman, he knew only too well; but only if he kept a cool head. And at this moment, it was anything but cool, for Howard's usual fluent style deserted him. Nevertheless, he fought with a determination and strength that might have forced a lesser man to acknowledge defeat. Charles kept his wits about him and never once faltered.

Deborah's hands were clasped tightly at her breast, her lower lip caught between her teeth. Osborne glanced at her. "Have no fear, Mistress Deborah," he said in a hurried undertone. "Should m'lord get the upper hand, I have something here that will stop him!" He tapped the pocket of his riding coat, unaware that Jackson was watching him and had, moreover perfectly understood the significance of the gesture. The man began to move cautiously towards him.

Howard was tiring. Sensing it, Charles pressed home his advantage, forcing him back; and then, with a swift, dexterous twist of the wrist, caught the point of his sword in the quillons of Howard's guard, wrenching the weapon from his grasp. Howard stood there, breathing heavily, his expression one of stunned disbelief.

Charles picked up the fallen weapon. "I win, I think."

Howard's lip curled. "By a low trick!"

"Trick or not, 'twas well done!" James came into the room, grinning broadly. "Danby and the others have just arrived."

"Good." Charles turned away. "I must take a look at Philip's arm."

Howard watched him go, and then gestured to Jackson to bring him his coat. The latter did so, helping him into it, and they exchanged a few muttered words.

Philip's wound having been tended, Charles declared it was time they left.

Howard eyed him levelly. "You're taking me back to London?"

"Where else? The sooner we make a start, the better. Are you ready?"

"Yes; but I'm not going with *you*! No, stay where you are!" This to James, who had gone impetuously forward to take his arm and now, to his surprise, found himself looking into the barrel of a pistol.

"Steady, James!" Charles warned quickly; and to Howard, "You've left nothing to chance, I see. I should have searched your pockets."

Howard smiled thinly. "You would not have found *this*. It came from another source." He glanced meaningly at Osborne, who started, clapped a hand to his own pocket and then assumed an expression of mortification.

"I see how it is, m'lord!" he exclaimed to Charles. "That villain Jackson took it from me without my knowledge, and gave it to his lordship."

Howard bowed mockingly. "Quite so. I would advise all of you to remain where you are. Except *you*, my sweet." He looked at Deborah. "Jackson!"

Deborah shrank back with a cry of alarm as the man swooped down upon her, but before he could touch her, Charles had hauled him away and sent him crashing to the floor.

"Keep your filthy hands off her!" he cried wrathfully.

There was a sudden exclamation from James. "Howard has gone!" He rushed over to the door in the panelling, only to find it locked.

Charles turned to Philip. "What lies behind that door?"

Philip frowned. "As I recall, a small room opening on to a passage, which in turn leads to a courtyard near the stables."

"I'll wager he had a horse ready there!" Charles cried. "Come along, James!"

They dashed out to their horses, Philip and Deborah following more slowly.

"There he goes!" called Charles. Howard, astride a powerful black stallion, was already approaching the open gates.

Charles flung himself up into his saddle and set off in hot pursuit, with James close behind.

"I fear they have little chance of catching him on *that* horse," Philip remarked, and then stopped with a sharp intake of breath.

A cumbersome, old-fashioned coach had suddenly turned in from the road. The coachman, occupied with controlling his team of four heavy Flanders horses as they manoeuvred the antiquated vehicle through the gateway, had no eyes for anything else. He did not notice Howard until it was too late.

The others saw the latter's frantic attempt to pull his horse's head round to avoid the collision, saw the black stallion rear up with a terrified scream, hooves flailing wildly – and then he was over, with Howard crushed beneath him.

Charles was the first to reach him. He bent over the inert form, then raised his head as James came up. "He's dead."

The coachman, white and shaking, managed to bring his frightened team to a halt in front of the house. The coach door opened and Helen appeared, her stricken gaze falling upon Philip, his arm in an improvised sling.

"Philip – I think Howard is dead! Did you see? And you... oh, my darling! Your arm!"

He went to her and, heedless of the others, put his uninjured arm round her. She clung to him and wept.

The old Marquis climbed painfully down from the coach and, finding Deborah beside him, patted her shoulder. "A bad business." He left her, to console his coachman.

She looked round. Philip had led Helen into the house. She walked a few paces along the avenue, and then halted. A figure detached itself from the little group surrounding Howard's body, and came towards her, head bent in thought. She waited until he was within earshot. Then – "Charles," she said softly, and held out her arms to him.

Masquerade
Historical Romances

Intrigue excitement romance

Don't miss
April's
other enthralling Historical Romance title

FOLLOW THE DRUM
by Judy Turner

The summer of 1815, when the drums of the Duke of Wellington's magnificent army are rolling across Europe . . . and in England the youthful Barbara Campion is faced with marriage to an elderly widower. Impulsively, she decides escape is the only answer and her childhood sweetheart, Harry, the only person who can help her. Disguising herself as a stable lad, she runs away to find Harry — in France with Wellington's army! Although her unit commander, the dashing Captain Daniel Alleyn, has his suspicions, Barbara's true identity remains a secret. But at the Ball on the eve of the Battle of Waterloo, she is forced out of her disguise on the orders of her commanding officer . . .

You can obtain this title today from your local paperback retailer

Doctor Nurse Romances

and April's
stories of romantic relationships behind the scenes
of modern medical life are:

PICTURE OF A DOCTOR
by Lisa Cooper

Doctor Luke Garner obviously considered Virginia a feckless, immoral artist, incapable of doing anything worthwhile. Why should she mind so much?

NURSE MARIA
by Marion Collin

Nurse Maria's love for Steven Ransome put her whole career in jeopardy. For Steven was her patient, and 'fraternisation' was strictly forbidden ...

Order your copies today from your local paperback retailer.

Masquerade
Historical Romances

Intrigue excitement romance

THE ELUSIVE MARRIAGE
by Patricia Ormsby

The scandalous circumstances of Cherryanne Devenish's first meeting with the notorious Marquis of Shalford made her anxious to forget the whole incident. Then she found that the more decorous courtships offered by other Regency bucks had lost their savour for her . . .

MARIA ELENA
by Valentina Luellen

A fragile pawn in her father's political game against Elizabeth I, Maria Elena was torn between loyalty to him and love for his mortal enemy, Adam MacDonald. And to Adam she was only an instrument of revenge!

Look out for these titles in your local paperback shop from 9th May 1980

Masquerade
Historical Romances

Intrigue excitement romance

MARIETTA
by Gina Veronese

Marietta was the richest woman in Florence — but when she fell in love with Filippo, poor but proud, she discovered that her wealth counted for nothing ... It could not recover his lost inheritance, or save them both from danger.

COUSIN CAROLINE
by Emma Gayle

Caroline Malbis had always idolised her dazzling Cousin Francis, but she had managed to keep her feelings under control. Would nursing Francis's invalid wife, near Victorian York, prove to be more than she could bear?

ABIGAIL'S QUEST
by Lois Mason

Abigail's father had disappeared — swallowed up in the gold rush to New Zealand in 1862. On her quest to look for him, she found herself married to Rob Sinclair — a near stranger!

These titles are still available through your local paperback retailer